Remember Me

CHAPEL COVE ROMANCES

WHEN LIFE BEGINS AT FORTY...

A Chapel Cove Romance
~ Book 1 ~

By

USA TODAY BESTSELLING AUTHOR

MARION UECKERMANN

Contact Information: marion.ueckermann@gmail.com

Scripture taken from Holy Bible, New International Version®, NIV® Copyright ©1973, 1978, 1984, 2011 by Biblica, Inc.® Used by permission. All rights reserved worldwide.

Cover Art by Marion Ueckermann: www.marionueckermann.net

Edited by Ailsa Williams.

Cover Image ID 213254156 Depositphotos © ArturVerkhovetskiy
Logo Image Chapel ID 164957864 Depositphotos © verity.cz

ISBN: 9781091173699

PRAISE FOR *Remember Me*

This story hits so many of my favorite themes, second chance for a love lost, chasing your life's dreams, and finding out God has an even better plan for us. Clarise and Heath have a love for each other that you can feel from the very beginning, but their timing has been off for years, until now. The "cast of secondary characters" are so engaging I cannot wait to read more about them!

~ Paula Marie, Blogger and Book Reviewer at Fiction Full of Faith

The ripple effects of bad choices can be devastating. Reese's story is one that many people can identify with. It is such an encouragement to see her claw her way back to purposeful living.

~ Ailsa Williams, Editor

Remember Me, is a wonderful story of love and hope. This author wrapped all this story in the wonderful message of God's love for us, even when we think our past is too bad. The setting for this book is in my favorite state of Oregon in a coastal town. Which, if you've never been, is so stunning! Marion Ueckermann is a gifted author. She blends together vivid pictures by her words to make all the scenes come to life. So much so, I started believing there really is a Chapel Cove, Oregon. (NOT!)

The characters in this story are written in such a way they are real and believable. I'd love to meet them. Some of the characters I really got a kick reading about. Aunt Ivy is one character who I'd love to meet. She's spunky and full of life.

Now, I can't forget to mention this tale also has some swoon-worthy moments. Reese and Heath have a hard time not heating up the scenes too much! But what's a romance novel without romance?

I will carry this story in my heart and smile when I think of it. I highly recommend you pick it up, also look for the next books in this series. I think we'll all love this piece of Oregon flair.

~ Marylin Furumasu, MF Literary Works

Marion Ueckermann writes books I love to read. They bring my heart comfort and put a smile on my face. *Remember Me* is a charming story full of wit and hummer. I laughed and cried my way through this marvelous story.

~ Renette Steele

Remember Me by Marion Ueckermann is a delightful Christian romance that will warm your heart. It is the first book in the Chapel Cove Romance series and I cannot wait for the subsequent books. The characters are delightful with warm and welcoming natures. Their interactions are wonderful to witness. Marion Ueckermann always creates characters that weave their way into the reader's heart.

I really enjoyed *Remember Me*. It was another fabulous offering from Marion Ueckermann. I always know that whenever I pick up any of her novels, I will be entertained, welcomed and left smiling, feeling good about the world.

Take a trip to Chapel Cove today, leave the world behind and relax for a few hours.

~ Julia Wilson, Book Reviewer at Christian Bookaholic

Very heartwarming, although sometimes heartbreaking, story filled with renewed hope of forgiveness, healing, trust, second chances, and new beginnings. The fictional town of Chapel Cove became so vivid in my mind that I wanted to linger in it, and even wished I could visit it in real life. Any reader can relate to wondering about the "what-if's" and the "why's" that are part of the characters' struggles in this story. A story that will capture your heart and imagination and will remain past the last word.

~ Becky Smith

I am always amazed and gratified with Marion's stories. Her grasp of human nature and how God figures in their lives makes her characters believable and lovable. With *Remember Me*, I fell in love with not just a couple, but an entire community. As soon as I can locate it on a map, I'm saving for a trip to Chapel Cove. Will you join me? I can hardly wait for the rest of this series.

~ Judith Robl, JR's Red Quill Editing, Author of *As Grandma Says*

Chapel Cove, Oregon....oh how Marion has created such a picturesque view of this quaint town with townsfolk that are as sweet as can be. I so wanna visit Chapel Cove and meet all the people. Reese and Heath are two I'd love to meet. These characters tied the whole story together with the hardships they overcome as life went on. Not letting fear drown their dreams, with tough love and finding faith in God, they pushed forward and battled those hardships to conquer the world and their lives.

~ Sharon Dean

As we traverse the valleys of life, "God, who is able to do more than we could ever ask or imagine" may not give us a do-over, but gives us second chances and hope. God's mercies are new every morning.

Remember Me is an inspiring start to the new Chapel Cove Romance series by Marion Ueckermann, Autumn Macarthur, and Alexa Verde. Marion weaves a twenty-seven year romance between Reese and Heath with life's heart breaking hiccups, second chances, and unexpected revelations into an intriguing page turning story. Does life begin at forty?

~ Renate Pennington, Retired English, Journalism, Creative Writing
High School Teacher

When Reese returns home she never expected to be happy again. Heath is an amazing man who has loved Reese forever. Watching these two try to get their lives together will have you on the edge of your seat waiting to see what happens next. You will feel God working throughout this wonderful inspirational story. I would give this book a higher rating than a five star review if I could.

~ Debbie Jamieson

This book is about a second chance at love after forty, with God's help. The story flows well with a strong cast of characters. This book is recommended for those who love Christian romance with an inspirational message.

~ Linda Rainey

Dear Reader

Not everyone gets a do-over—
a chance to rectify
wrong actions,
wrong choices,
wrong turns.

God is able to use our failures for good and
bring beauty out of the ashes of regret.

If you are in need of a second chance,
you'll find it at the nail-scarred feet of God's only son,
Jesus.

Be blessed,

Marion

To Ann Ellison ~

I miss you reading my stories.

Husbands, love your wives,
just as Christ loved the church
and gave himself up for her.

~ Ephesians 5:25 (NIV)

PROLOGUE

Friday, April 12

SEATED CROSS-LEGGED on the floor of her bedroom with her two best friends, Clarise Aylward leaned forward and lit the candles on the birthday cake her mom had made for them. As if conducting a choir, she lifted her hands in the air and the three girls sang together merrily, heads bopping and bodies swaying as their voices filled the room.

"Happy birthday to us. Happy birthday to us. Happy birthday to u-u-s. Happy birthday to us."

With a unified breath, they blew out the thirteen candles balancing on white, plastic candleholders, shaped like flowers, which were pegged into the pink frosting. Clapping their hands with excitement, they cheered. How awesome it was that their birthdays were days apart and they could celebrate together every year.

"Are we women now? Or at least, will we be after we've all had our birthdays?" asked Kristina, the youngest by a day, although her petite frame compared to Clarise and Naomi's lankier lengths made her look far younger.

Naomi turned to her. "I don't know. Don't girls only become women when they get their —" A ruddy hue colored her cheeks. She adjusted her glasses, her eyes exaggerated behind the thick lenses. "Well, you know..."

"Hah, if that were the case, I'd have been a woman months ago." Kristina swung her stick-straight hair over her shoulder. "And I don't know how someone who hasn't even become a teenager could be a woman."

Poor Kristina, it was the Latino's curse to have her periods way earlier than most.

A giggle slipped from Clarise's lips. "My mom sat me down last week to speak to me about it. She said it was time I knew as she had started her—" Cheeks warming, she glanced at Kristina for some backup. She got nothing except an impatient stare.

Clarise sucked in a deep breath, feeling as embarrassed to say the word out loud in front of her friends as Naomi had seemingly been. "Well, you know what started, and that was shortly after she became a teenager. I just let her talk...didn't have the heart to tell her we'd already been taught all that stuff at school."

"I missed that class." Naomi's mouth turned down on one side. "When Kristina told us after it happened to her, I went and read up about it at the school library. There was no way I could ask *my* mom."

Kristina reached out and squeezed Naomi's arm. "I could've told you more. You should have asked."

Naomi shrugged.

"Ugh, well if that's the rite of passage to womanhood, it doesn't seem as if being a woman will be that much fun." Clarise pursed her lips and shook her head. "So, I think I'll just stay thirteen for the rest of my life."

A loud snort tumbled out of Kristina's mouth. "You know that's not possible. Besides, think of all those 'sweet sixteen' kisses you'll miss out on one day if you *could* stay thirteen." She bumped her shoulder against Clarise's, sending the piece of cake Clarise was plating for herself tumbling onto the carpet.

Clarise shot Kristina an annoyed glare. "Now look what you've done." She lifted the slice onto the plate and picked out a few carpet hairs that had stuck to the topping. Eyeing the rest of the uncut cake, Clarise dragged her index finger through the frosting then smeared her finger across Kristina's cheek, leaving a thick, gooey, pink stripe in its wake.

"Clarise! Ooh, now you've asked for it." Scrambling to her knees, the smallest of the friends returned the favor and colored Clarise's chin with the sweet, pink warpaint.

Quickly, Naomi joined in the fun, and soon all three girls were rolling on the floor, giggling and looking as if they'd sneaked one of the face masks from Clarise's mom's beauty products.

When their laughter finally subsided, Clarise sat up and examined the cake. The only pieces still intact, were the three she'd plated before the frosting fight began—and that only because someone had shown the presence of mind to move them under her desk, out of the way.

Before *those* were also used as ammunition, Clarise leaned forward, stretching for her plate. She grabbed the cake and shoved it into her mouth, biting off a huge chunk.

"Good idea." Torso twisting, Naomi reached behind her for the other two plates. She handed one to Kristina and the two girls followed Clarise's lead with moans of delight.

3

While Clarise chewed, she wiped the frosting from her face, dropping pink dollops back onto her plate. Running her tongue over her teeth, she tried to loosen the cake that had stuck to her braces. She couldn't wait for those silvery tracks to be removed from her teeth. Unfortunately, she'd be fifteen before she tasted freedom.

Once they'd finished eating their cake, the trio rushed out of the bedroom in a flurry of giggles, down the passage, and into the bathroom to wash the stickiness from their faces and hands. Then they filed back to Clarise's bedroom, their giggles once again trailing in their wake. One by one, they flopped onto the double bed, but not before making sure the bowl of potato chips followed them.

And their pop.

Hands beneath her head, Naomi stared up at the ceiling and sighed. "You're so lucky to have such a big bed, Clarise."

"Well, not so lucky when family come to visit because then I have to sleep on the sofa downstairs." But they didn't have family too often and the big bed had come in handy for all their slumber parties, although the three of them didn't fit quite as well as they had when they were little girls. One of these days, they'd have to pull out the inflatable mattress and draw straws for who got to sleep on it.

Maybe even tonight.

Every year since they'd turned seven—old enough for sleepovers according to their parents—they'd celebrated their birthdays at Clarise's house on the preceding Friday. Kristina's parents were too poor to host the sleepovers, and Naomi's mom...well, she was just too mean. Frankly, she frightened Clarise, so Clarise didn't mind at all that her mom and dad loved hosting the annual birthday celebrations. Maybe they'd wanted a bigger family, but instead, they only had her.

Leaning over the side of the bed, Clarise's hand swept the carpet under the bed until her fingers latched onto the two small gifts she'd hidden there earlier. She drew them into her palm.

Seated upright again, she handed one to Naomi and one to Kristina, offering them a wide smile. "Happy birthday. Just a little something I made for each of you."

Naomi sat up.

Kristina stared at the gift in her hands. "Clarise, you shouldn't have. You know I can't—"

"Kris, stop. How many times do I have to tell you that I don't expect a gift in return? Besides, it didn't cost me anything except a few hours of my time."

Probably guessing the gifts were the same, her friends rushed to open theirs first. Fortunately, the wrappings ripped at exactly the same time and the shell bracelets tumbled simultaneously onto the bedcovers.

Kristina lifted hers, holding it up to the light to examine each intricate shell that Clarise had joined together.

Naomi slid her bracelet onto her wrist. Extending her arm, she gazed at the piece of jewelry for a moment before bringing her arm to her chest. She traced a finger over the hard seashells. "These are beautiful, Clarise. Thanks. You should think about becoming a jewelry designer when you grow up. You're really good at it. You could sell them down at the boardwalk."

Clarise waved away her suggestion, wrinkling her nose. "Nah. When I grow up, I want to be a supermodel." She reached for the magazine on the nightstand and dropped it face up on the bed between them. Cindy Crawford smiled back from the glossy cover of Vogue. "Just like her."

Kristina chuckled. "Right, Clarise. With those zits and braces? Besides, you're way too skinny and lanky."

Lips pursed and nostrils flaring ever so slightly, Clarise held back her retort, not wanting to get into an argument on their birthday celebration day. She jutted out her chin. "Models are supposed to be tall and thin. And my braces and zits won't last forever." Anyway, she didn't have *that* many skin blemishes. Just a few here and there. Normal teen stuff. It would pass.

She glanced across to Naomi. "Hey, your mom enrolled you in every local beauty pageant since before you could walk, maybe she could give me some pointers?"

Naomi's shoulders lifted in a shrug. "My mother doesn't like to help anyone but herself, unfortunately. Besides, Mom's interest in beauty pageants vanished when I lost all that baby cuteness, packed on some pounds, and needed glasses. Not to mention my teeth that decided to grow horizontally, not vertically. Plus, like you, Clarise, I also suffered the curse of the spots."

"What's this? Pick on Clarise's spots day?" Clarise snapped. *Sheesh.* She only had the occasional outbreak.

Trying to make light of the fact that she'd gotten annoyed so easily, Clarise chuckled. "It's not like I have to take Accutane for them or anything else as drastic."

Naomi eased down onto her stomach, feet hanging in the air as her body ran out of mattress. "You know what we should do? We should write up a list of things we want to achieve before we're twenty, and then—"

"Twenty! Nobody achieves much in life before they're twenty," Kristina protested. "Make it thirty."

"Why not forty?" Clarise offered. "Mom turned forty last year and she keeps saying that life only begins at forty."

Naomi pulled the magazine closer and flipped through the pages. "Okay, forty it is. How about ten things we want to achieve by the time we're forty?"

"Can we make it five?" Kristina's gaze skipped between Clarise and Naomi. "It's just…well, I'm at a bit of a disadvantage, being poor and all—"

Naomi closed the magazine and set it down on the bed. "Mom and I aren't that flush either." She reached for the chips and, grabbing a handful, popped them into her mouth one at a time.

Kristina's shoulders lifted as she drew in a deep breath then slumped with her exhale. "I would rather have fewer things to achieve and feel good about achieving what I set out to do. I don't want to have a bunch of regrets when I get to forty. What way would that be to start out life, *if* life actually begins at forty as your mom says?" She directed her question at Clarise.

Clarise hopped off the bed and trotted over to her desk to snatch up her writing pad and a pen from the wooden surface. She returned to her friends and stretched out across the bottom end of the bed. Pressing the pen to the paper, she began to write.

WHAT I PLAN TO ACHIEVE BY THE TIME I'M FORTY.

"Who's going first?" Kristina asked.

Naomi rolled over and snuggled into the pillows, clearly not eager to be elected.

Clarise raised her hand, pointing the pen toward the ceiling. "I will, seeing as I've already said what I want to be one day. Plus, I have the writing implements."

She moved the pen over the paper again, speaking each word out loud as she wrote. "Number one. I will be a famous model." She crossed out the word model then added, "Supermodel."

"Shooting a little high, aren't you, Clarise?" Kristina lifted one eyebrow.

"Well, if I aim for Jupiter, I might just hit Venus…" Clarise shook her head. "Or something like that."

Naomi giggled. "The stars, silly, but everyone knows they're trillions of miles away, so no good aiming for them."

Clarise pointed her finger at her friend and winked. "Exactly. And by the way, I've decided that you can call me Reese from now on. If I had my way, I'd change my surname too. It would stop that bully, Olivia Patterson, from calling me Awkward instead of Aylward."

Head of the cheerleading squad, perky Olivia with her bouncing blond curls made all the plain Janes' lives a living hell.

Lowering her head to the mattress, Clarise bumped it a few times against the soft surface. "Agh, as if my surname weren't enough to deal with, what were my parents thinking giving me a name where, when people say it, their minds are immediately drawn to a scene from *The Silence of the Lambs*?"

Naomi shot upright, eyes wide, and gasped. "You've seen *The Silence of the Lambs*?"

Smacking the back of her hand against Naomi's leg, Clarise squealed, "Of course not!"

Naomi eyed her, questions filling her pointed stare. "Well then how do you know so much about the movie?"

"I don't know *much* about the movie. It's just—" Clarise huffed as heat warmed her cheeks. She'd opened herself up to this conversation, and now there was no going back. "Heath from the eleventh grade keeps teasing me, saying 'Helloooo, Clarise' in this deep voice every time he sees me."

"Heath Brock? That Heath?" Without pausing for a breath, Naomi's questions persisted. "The one whose little brother, Hudson, joined our class last year?"

Clarise pressed her palms to her temple, twining her fingers together on the top of her head. *Mercy, give me a break!* Granted the Brock family had only been in Chapel Cove for a couple of months now, but how many Heath Brocks could there possibly be in their little town? Of course the same one, whom, hopefully, Naomi didn't have some crush on.

Not that Clarise did.

Did she?

8

Come to think of it, whenever Heath came near, her heart *did* thump in her chest.

Actually, it more like whacked against her ribcage. Sometimes so hard, it hurt.

Drawing in a deep breath, Clarise doodled a little flower in the corner of the page as she nonchalantly replied, "The very one."

She glanced at the sketch, breathing a sigh of relief that she hadn't gone and absent-mindedly drawn a heart with an arrow through it. She set the pen down before she got carried away.

"When I asked him why he keeps doing that," Clarise continued, "he said, 'Have you never seen *The Silence of the Lambs*?'" She blew out air through her lips. "What a jerk."

"I wouldn't know. But if he is, he's rather a cute jerk. Although I'm sure you've noticed that." Kristina chuckled as she raised an eyebrow. "Hudson's cute too. Hey, maybe Heath likes you, and that's why he's teasing you."

Clarise rolled her eyes. "Pfft. Right... As if someone like him would want something like this for a girlfriend." Pointing her finger, she circled her face. "Besides, I'm three years younger—not exactly the type of girl someone like Heath would go for."

Naomi reached over and brushed her hand over Clarise's. "I think you're pretty. And you've got such beautiful, long, strawberry-blond hair. I wish my hair was that color instead of this..." She lifted a lock of her hair and stared at it, dissatisfaction scribbled across her face. "Blah black."

Kristina laughed. "Blah black? Is that even a color?"

"Whatever..." came Naomi's response. She lifted a thick strand of hair. "And if this color isn't enough, just look at how straight it is—all those gorgeous baby curls I'd once had are long gone."

"Clarise, don't sell yourself short for any guy," Kristina continued. "You're not only pretty, as Naomi said, and you've got all that hair and long legs going for you, but you're also caring and so much fun to be with. I'm glad that you're my friend."

Naomi's hand shot up into the air. "Me too."

Not one for compliments, Clarise muttered, "Okay, okay, enough gushing. Back to Mr. Brock. How did he get to see the film anyway? He's only sixteen, and that movie carries an R rating."

"Well…" Arms crossed, Naomi tapped a finger against her lips as if she was about to say something quite profound. "Heath and Hudson *do* have an older brother who left school last year. I guess he's eighteen or so. I've seen them all around the trailer park where I live. I think their uncle owns it *and* the RV resort down at the beach. At least, they have the same surname. Anyway, the older brother is just as handsome. He's probably the one who rented the movie and let Heath watch it."

"Rented? I doubt it. Hasn't it just released in the cinemas?" Fingers to her chin, Clarise tapped her lips with her index finger. "Unless he and his older brother snuck into a cinema in Portland. Heath *could* pass as a little older than he actually is."

Kristina's eyes widened. "What if they somehow got their hands on a pirated copy of the film?"

"Well, if that's the case, I hope they had the sense not to let Hudson watch as well." Clarise huffed. "Seriously, doesn't their mother discipline them?"

Kristina reached for her pop standing on the nightstand nearest her. Wrapping her lips around the straw, she took a long sip. "Actually, I don't think they have a mother. I've only heard Hudson speak about his father. And I've never seen Heath and Hudson at church with anyone but their dad—the few times they've been there."

Watching Kristina quench her thirst reminded Clarise that she was pretty parched too. Rising, she arched her back in a stretch, then pattered over to her desk where she'd left her drink.

Her thirst quenched, Clarise set the can down on the carpet just under the bed where it wouldn't get knocked over and perched herself on the edge of the mattress. "That explains a lot then. Poor guys. Without a mother, one has to wonder if those Brock boys will amount to anything."

"And we will?" Kristina asked, that brow of hers raised once again. "Living in Chapel Cove, Oregon? Population 6304?"

Clarise squared her shoulders. "Speak for yourself. I will."

Kristina dug her hand into the chip bowl, her laughter rushing to the ceiling. "Right...I forgot, you're going to be a famous supermodel when you're older."

"I am! And I'll travel the world, wear fancy jewelry and clothes, and I'll be on the covers of all those glossy magazines we love looking at. It's my dream, and I *will* make it happen."

"Why do you have to dream so big, Clarise...I mean Reese?" Naomi blew out a huff. "This is going to take some getting used to. I mean, at the moment you're pretty much an—"

"Ugly duckling?" As if Naomi had room to talk. Clarise tipped her chin a fraction. "You've heard the story of the swan. Well, that's going to be me. Two more years and these braces come off. So just watch this space."

"Ooh, then you'll be Heath Brock material." Kristina giggled. "Write this one on your list. Before I'm forty, although maybe we should make that fourteen, I will kiss Heath Brock."

"I'm not writing that on my list!" The way her voice had just risen three pitches surprised Clarise. Besides, she would never want her first kiss to happen while she was, as Olivia Patterson called her, "Jaws"—and that reference was to Ian Fleming's steel-capped-teeth-hoodlum in the 007 movie, not the lead creature in Spielberg's shark movie. Although, knowing Olivia, she probably meant both.

"Oh yes, you are!" Kristina grabbed the paper and pen and wrote in big letters, I WILL KISS HEATH BROCK.

Naomi and Kristina's shrieks filled the room.

"Although of course I'd prefer it if you married Roman," Kristina quickly added. "We'd be family then."

Clarise squealed in protest as she tried to retrieve her list before Kristina added marriage to her twin brother as well. "Give me that." She snatched back the pen and paper. She was about to scratch out what Kristina had written then decided against it. Who knew, maybe she *would* get to kiss Heath Brock before she was forty. Besides, it gave her ammunition to get revenge on her two friends.

Her eyes narrowed as she stared down at Naomi and Kristina. "You both just wait until it's your turn to make *your* lists. I'm going to give you an equally awful one to write down."

Not that the idea of kissing Heath was at all repulsive.

But she'd better get her list finished before her friends came up with any more crazy notions.

Clarise scribbled and spoke furiously. "Number three—I will have a husband who loves and adores me. Number four—I will have a baby, maybe two or three. Number five—I will live a life sold out for Jesus, because without Him my mom says, you can achieve nothing." She scrunched up her nose. "I probably should have made that number one."

Clarise scribbled out the numbers then renumbered the list before tearing the sheet from the gummed edge. She shoved the pen and pad over to Naomi. "There. Done. Your turn." She folded her paper twice, then wrote her name diagonally across the small, neat square.

Naomi stared at the writing utensil as if the pen was a snake, about to strike. "I–I need more time to think. Kristina, you go next."

With an eye roll, Kristina snatched up the pen and paper. "What are we going to do with these lists, anyway? By the time we're forty, the papers will likely be lost and we'll probably have forgotten what we'd written."

Clarise shot to her feet and returned to her desk. She knew exactly what they could do to safeguard the security of their pledges. Reaching up to the shelf above her desk, she took down a square tin that had once housed the most delicious chocolate chip cookies ever made. Mom had wanted to throw out the container, but Clarise liked the tin so she'd asked her mother if she could keep it for odds and ends. So far all it had gathered over the months was dust.

She blew the dust bunnies from the metal surface before opening the tin and dropping it on the bed. "Why don't we put them in here? Tomorrow morning, we can ride our bikes up to the chapel on the cove and bury it somewhere near there. Let's make a promise that once we've all turned forty, no matter where in the world we find ourselves, we'll meet up here again to unearth our buried treasure."

Naomi clapped her hands together. "That's a great idea! Something like a time capsule."

"W-e-l-l...of a sort, but not really," Kristina quipped. "Not much of a buried treasure though, if there are only going to be these three lists in the tin."

And she was right. They needed something more substantial inside that tin.

Clarise's breath hitched. "I know. Why don't we each put a special, personal item inside the tin? Something we'd like to get back one day?"

Kristina's eyes brightened with excitement. "That's a great idea, Cl— Reese. But we'll have to go past my house first tomorrow so that I can get something."

Naomi stuck her hand into the air again. "Me too, although I'm not quite sure what to put inside the tin." She shrugged. "Meh, I'll think of something. I have all night."

"Don't lose any sleep." With a chuckle, Kristina softly shoved at Naomi's shoulder.

"Of course we'll go past your houses first." Clarise grinned and rose. "Thankfully, I won't need to lose any sleep over this, because I know exactly what I want to put inside that tin."

CHAPTER ONE

Twenty-seven years later…

THE ACRID smell of cigarettes and dust seemed to overpower Reese Aylward even more than when she'd stepped inside the dingy pawn shop a few minutes ago. If it wasn't for the distasteful task set before her, she would've dashed right out again into the New York mayhem.

Mouth dry, her heart pounded uncontrollably—partly from fear of the future, partly from anger over the past. Mostly though, it broke for what could and should never have been. Now, more than ever, she longed for the peace and quiet of home, far away on the opposite side of America.

Chapel Cove.

She closed her eyes and allowed an image of pristine beaches, a red and white lighthouse up on the cliff, and the tiny, old chapel she and her friends used to explore to fill her mind and calm her. For a brief moment, waves crashed onto the shore and seagulls hovered above the churning surf, blotting out the sound of the middle-aged owner's heavy breathing.

Her eyes flew open at the recollection of where she was and what she was about to do. Hands to her hips, Reese stared at the man—Mr. Payne according to the signage outside his questionable establishment—her unbelief challenging him. Not that he seemed to care. Clearly a ruthless businessman, knowing a bargain and a desperate woman when he saw one and having no compassion for the latter, his focus remained fixed on the diamond ring that sparkled under the scrutiny of the bright light strapped to his forehead. Dust mites floated in the path of the beam.

This was an insult! She'd worn that ring for exactly fifteen years. Lloyd had taken her to Tiffany's on 5th Avenue that Valentine's Day and told her to choose whatever rock her little heart desired. And then, sliding the two carat cushion-cut engagement ring with a pavé-set diamond band onto her finger, he'd proposed, promising her his undying love.

Right… It wasn't even two years before he was chasing the next pretty skirt. And he never stopped. Unfortunately, as co-owner of one of New York's top modelling agencies, he saw a lot of those pretty skirts. Reese wouldn't be surprised if he'd been unfaithful from the moment their honeymoon was over. She'd just been too stupid to notice it before. And even more stupid not to have done something about it for thirteen long years. Oh, she'd cried, she'd thrown tantrums—but that wasn't enough to make her wandering husband stop. Well, she was done with Lloyd Barkley and his posh British accent, empty promises, and lying ways. This past Christmas Eve she'd walked out and filed for a divorce.

But enough of her cheating ex-husband. Currently she had

another cheating man to deal with. If only she could walk out on this one too, but she needed the money. Fast. If she could've sold her rings at a reputable jewelry store, she would have. But Lloyd seemed to have friends all over this city, in all sorts of places. Except places such as where she presently found herself. She didn't want him preventing her from selling her engagement and wedding rings in the same way he'd blocked so many job opportunities for her these past seven weeks.

He had wanted, no demanded, the rings back. She'd refused. They were hers, and they were the one thing that could give her a new start back home, seeing as Lloyd had swindled her out of most of her earnings, not to mention railroading her career. And now it seemed her fresh beginning wouldn't be as bright and easy as she'd hoped.

The pawnbroker cleared his throat, looking up at Reese as he turned off the light on the headband magnifier and lifted the visor out of the way. He set the diamond ring down on the velvet cloth beside her matching platinum wedding band. "Well?"

Pursing her lips, Reese sucked in a deep breath. She knew the ring's worth—Lloyd had revalued it only a few months back for insurance purposes—and it was worth way, way more than—

"Five thousand dollars? Are you crazy? That ring is worth eight times that!"

Mr. Payne splayed his fingers over the dusty, wooden counter beside the velvet square. He shrugged. "Choice is yours. Take it or leave it. And I only keep goods for one month. If you don't come back to reclaim the rings, they'll become mine to do with as I wish."

Like she would come back to New York to claim those rings. She was done with this city. She was done with her career. And she was certainly done with her husband.

Although she hated to let the jewelry go for so little, what choice did she have? The sooner she headed back to the west coast, the better.

"Fine." She thumped her palms down hard on the counter. "And the wedding band?"

"Five thousand for both."

Wha–? He was as cruel and cunning as her ex.

"Five five," she ventured. Another few hundred dollars could buy her a plane ticket home to Oregon and pay for her rental car from Portland to Chapel Cove.

Without a word, Mr. Payne pivoted and walked back into his office just behind the counter. He shut the door.

Reese bit down on her lip. She shouldn't have pushed for the extra cash.

"Wait…" she started with a whisper as she reached out, then stopped. He couldn't just leave her standing there. What went out had to come back in. Maybe she should stride over to that front door, open and close it—twice—pretending she was going out and another customer coming in moments later. That should draw the shrewd little weasel back out of hiding.

Before she could execute her plan, the office door opened and Mr. Payne stepped back to the counter, a wad of notes clasped between his grubby fingers. Without looking at Reese, he started to count the money in front of her, right up until the last dollar. "Five thousand, five hundred," he said as he set the last note on top of the others. The dour look on his face and his downturned lips bore witness to his displeasure at having to part with an extra five hundred dollars. Too bad. Extra money or not, he still got the bargain of the century.

Reese grabbed the notes and stuffed them into her designer handbag. Without offering a farewell greeting, or taking a second look at those rings, she whirled around and marched out of the pawn shop. As she stepped outside, Reese paused for a final look at the signage on the store front.

PAYNE'S PAWNBROKING

WE PAY WHAT IT'S WORTH!

The heck they did.

Bile rose in her throat as she stared at her bare fingers. Her eyes stung, and not from the biting cold. She quickly fastened her jacket, then pulled on her woolen hat and gloves, an overwhelming sense of loss filling her. But Mr. Payne was just another thorn in Reese Aylward's side. She'd had more than one of those to deal with in her life—men using her for their own selfish gain.

Swallowing hard, Reese straightened her shoulders back to walk taller and strode with purpose down the sidewalk. She had survived then, and she'd certainly survive now.

Perspiration making his running pants cling to his legs, Heath Brock toed his shoes from his feet. Leaving them on the beach sand outside his camper, he stepped inside the cramped living quarters, his arm already stretching for the small refrigerator beside the narrow door. He opened it and pulled out a bottle of sparkling water, downing the contents in a few thirsty gulps before grabbing another to enjoy at a more leisurely pace.

Plopping down in the doorway, his socked feet perched on the portable, metal step that led into the camper, Heath wiped his brow against his sweatshirt then rested his elbows on his thighs. He stared across the beach and the ocean as he sipped from the bottle. He was one lucky man. Granted, he might be living in teensy-weensy accommodation, but he most certainly must have the best view in all of Chapel Cove. If he were any closer to the shore, he'd be stepping out of his camper onto wet sand every time the tide came in.

Pfft. Lucky? Really? What's so lucky about living the life of a hermit? Or rather, a monk?

Well...monk-like. But he'd had his brief moment in the sun.

Every year, on this particular day when love was so thick in the air you could smell the pheromones, doubts about his life choices invariably taunted him. What normal man spent Valentine's Day on his own, year after year? One would think that at forty-three he would've become accustomed to it.

Nope. He missed having a woman to love.

He missed her. His Clarise...or Reese as she'd insisted on being called the moment she'd turned thirteen.

Man, that girl had spunk. And he had loved her from the very moment his eyes first met her amber gaze. Then when five long years later he finally managed to invite her out, he'd ruined it. They'd had but one date, one Valentine's together, and it had changed everything. What foolish choices he'd made that night so long, long ago. Twenty-two years to be exact.

Time had not diminished his love for Reese. He still loved her, even though he knew he shouldn't. Unfortunately, he probably always would.

It was his fault, all his doing, that she had left Chapel Cove. But then, Reese was such a strong-willed dreamer, he probably would never have been able to keep her tied to this tiny town. Chapel Cove was way too small for Clarise Aylward. So perhaps it was for the best that things between them had crashed and burned at lightning speed. Reese had achieved so much that he could never have given her.

One question haunted him though—was she happy? Because at the end of the day, that's the only thing that really mattered.

He hoped she was. He truly did.

And from the photos he'd seen of her splashed on magazine covers all these years, it did seem as if she was. But then, a photo can paint a totally different picture than reality.

CHAPTER TWO

REESE SHUFFLED into the kitchen, pulling the gown Mom had lent her tighter around her waist. She looked up to see her mother standing in front of the stove, hands on her hips.

Mom glared at her.

Uh-oh. Reese knew that look—there'd be no escaping the lecture that was about to follow.

"Clarise Barkley! You've been—"

"Aylward, Mom. I haven't been a Barkley since Valentine's Day when my divorce become final." How Lloyd had managed to push it through that fast was beyond her. Clearly his reach in New York City extended further than she'd thought. It was a miracle he hadn't contested it, but then he had married again the very same day he'd gotten back the freedom he so craved.

No doubt in her mind now that the leggy blonde—young

enough to be his daughter—had been the reason he'd craved it.

Well, she could have him and all the drama that came along with being Mrs. Barkley.

Reese poured herself a cup of strong coffee then slumped into a chair at the kitchen table. She peered at her mother over the rim of the mug before lowering it. "And it's Reese. You know that."

Mom shook her gray head slowly and closed her eyes. When she opened them, they glistened with moisture. "You'll always be my Clarise," she said softly. "But I'll try to remember."

Easing down into the chair beside her, Mom took Reese's hand and offered her a weak smile. "I'm worried about you, baby. After not coming home for five years, you arrive unannounced on our doorstep seven weeks ago and tell us you're divorced. And you've barely left the house since then. Goodness, Reese, your father and I didn't even know your marriage was in trouble."

Oh yes, she and Lloyd had hidden it well the times that Reese had flown her parents across the country for visits.

Seeing her mother's angst, a lump formed in Reese's throat. Her eyes stung as she blinked back the tears. "I–I didn't want to worry you, Mom. I hoped…prayed…that things would change. They didn't." And who could blame God for not listening to her prayers? She hadn't lived in His will since she was nearly eighteen.

She sighed. "Finally, I couldn't take it any longer, and I walked out."

Mom squeezed her hand. "Oh darling child, if I could whisk away your pain, I would."

Mom's gaze shifted to the table, and then slowly returned to Reese. "D–did he abuse you?"

Reese shook her head. Thankfully, lifting his hand to her was one thing Lloyd Barkley was never guilty of. Probably only because he couldn't risk damaging his merchandise. Her face and body were worth more to him than giving in to a moment's rage.

But when she'd turned her back on him and he could no longer make money from her, he did everything in his power to ruin her.

The day after Reese had walked out on Lloyd, he'd changed the locks. She couldn't return for any of her clothes or jewelry. He had her car taken away from her as it was registered under his name—yet another of his expensive gifts to ease his guilty conscience. She'd had to rely on public transportation. After weeks of trying to get another job, Reese finally had to admit defeat and make the tough decision to return to Chapel Cove with just over five thousand dollars to her name and trailing the single suitcase of clothes she'd walked out of their Manhattan apartment with after her and Lloyd's Christmas Eve dinner guests had left. Lloyd had disappeared soon after with the leggy blonde who had stuck to him the entire night like a leech. Bambi, or Barbie, or something like that. Oh, she'd had a few choice "B" words herself for the woman.

Reese filled her lungs, then exhaled slowly as she stared into her mother's eyes. "Lloyd cheated on me. For years. It took me two years to discover the first affair. I–I was so stupid to believe his lies. I suspect he hadn't remained faithful for very long after our wedding. Eventually, he didn't even try to hide it. I think the only reason he wanted to marry me is because I wouldn't fall into bed with him like other models had done." She'd made that same mistake once with someone. And the day she left Chapel Cove—all of eighteen years old—Reese had promised herself that she would never again be guilty of the same lapse of judgment.

Finger to the porcelain mug, Reese traced the heart pattern on the warm surface. "Lloyd always wanted whatever he couldn't have. I–I was just one of those things on his list…for a while at least."

Mom's soft gaze searched hers as she cupped Reese's cheek. "I'm so sorry. He'd always seemed like such a charming man. I can't believe—"

"The serpent was a charmer too, Mom, and look where that got mankind. Eve might've been the first woman to be blinded by a snake's lies, but she certainly wasn't the last. Neither am I. But I will never again allow myself to be fooled by a man's sweet words."

"Not all men are like your ex-husband, Reese." Mom rose and grabbed the loaf of bread from the refrigerator. "Toast?"

Reese nodded. She was starving.

Mom popped four slices in the extra-large toaster then turned back to Reese. "Why don't you come to church with Dad and me on Sunday? We have a wonderful youth pastor now, although he's already been there for almost five years. He's doing an amazing job with our teens. He's your age *and* single." Mom shook her head. "Hard to believe someone so ruggedly good-looking hasn't been snapped up by some woman yet. The two of you would get along very well, I'm sure. Maybe you can be the one to win his heart."

Reese's eyes widened.

Seriously? Was her mom really trying to set her up with someone? And not just anyone...a preacher to boot?

"E–even if just as friends, honey," Mom pleaded. "You need other people in your life, Reese, not just Dad and me."

Reese pursed her lips for a moment. "I see what you're trying to do, Mom, and although I'm grateful that you're looking out for me, I'm not interested in replacing my husband. Not now. Not ever."

"Well then at least call Kristina, catch up with her. She's been back in town for three weeks already and you've yet to contact her. You girls are still all friends, aren't you? You were so inseparable through childhood."

"Of course we are. We'll be friends forever. But I— I just can't. Not now. I'm not ready to tell them about my divorce." Her chest heaved. "But I will...soon."

The toast popped up, and Mom removed the four slices and set them down in a basket, cocooning them in a tea towel. She shifted the basket, tub of butter, and bottles of jam onto the table, then lifted Reese's empty cup. "Refill?"

Reese shot her a grin. "Yes, please. Where's Dad? I thought he'd be down by now?"

"He needed to pop out to the hardware store. He'll be here soon, I'm sure. But let's not wait." Mom refilled the cup with the dark brew then handed it back to Reese, offering a tentative smile. "Sugarlump, you're far too young to shut yourself off from love. And life."

Mom lowered her gaze, seemingly unable to look into Reese's eyes. The toast she buttered afforded her a plausible excuse. "Your father and I have been talking, a–and we both agree that you can't mope around here all day long doing nothing but watching TV and feeding your face. As much as we love having you here with us again, baby girl, we need to exercise tough love…for your own good. So, no more mooching. We're giving you one month to get your life back on track. That means you need to find a job and you need to find your own place."

Reese's eyes widened and her jaw dropped in disbelief. "You're kicking me out?"

Staring at Reese, Mom's mouth curved in a grin. "Like a mamma bird. You've spread your wings and flown before, Reese—and my, how high you did fly. We know you can do it again."

All day long, her mother's words had bothered Reese. She couldn't believe Mom and Dad were kicking her out. One month to pull herself together? Not a lot of time, considering she'd been in a kind of depressive fog for seven weeks. She hadn't even breathed a word to Kristina and Naomi, or Nai as she'd decided to call herself the day after Clarise had announced her own name change. As far as her friends knew, Reese was still alive and well in New York City.

Why had her divorce hit her so hard the moment she got back home? It wasn't as if she still loved Lloyd. No, those feelings had died a long time ago, and sometimes she wondered if she'd ever really loved him. Had he truly been her soulmate?

Clearly not.

Suddenly, the walls of her room began to close in on her. She had to get out of there. She'd go for a walk. But not in her sweatpants.

Reese flung open her closet and reached for one of the three pairs of jeans she owned. She slid it off the hanger. She hadn't worn jeans in weeks.

Reese dropped her sweatpants to the floor. She stepped inside the denim, the fabric hugging her slender legs. Pulling up the jeans, she tried to fasten them. What the—? No way would she get that little button through its buttonhole. Not even close. Even the zipper only went up half way.

She fell back onto the bed with a groan, sucked in her stomach, and tried the zip again.

Nope. Even that didn't help.

How had she let herself go like this? Lloyd would have fired her.

She began to laugh hysterically because, in a way, he had.

Maybe Mom was right. Sitting around all day with no exercise and eating junk food had piled on the extra pounds, although it didn't take much flab to make those skintight pants unwearable. Well, her folks might feel the need to exercise tough love, but she just needed to exercise, period. Thankfully her jogging pants and running shoes had landed in her suitcase the night she'd walked out on Lloyd.

Needing to escape, to get back in shape, to clear her mind, Reese changed into the black lycra pants. The fabric wrapped around her legs like a second skin. She grabbed her Nike's from the closet, slid her feet inside, and laced them up.

After pulling on a cerise pink T-shirt, she donned her favorite black hoodie. The April temperatures were still way too fresh to go outside without wearing something warm, although, depending on how hard she ran, she might find herself shedding that piece of clothing on the way. Now all she had to still do was tie up her hair into a ponytail and those athletic shoes could hit the asphalt.

Still recovering from the morning's basketball session with the troubled youths he worked with, Heath stepped inside his camper and flopped onto his bed. He would've loved a cup of coffee, but he was way too tired to make one. Maybe after he had a power nap.

Power nap? In the middle of a Saturday afternoon? Man, he was getting old. It had to be true what they said, that it's all downhill after forty. Forget the idea that life began at forty. He didn't believe that for a single moment.

But if expending all his energy with a bunch of sixteen-year-olds would show them the way to Jesus and prevent them from ruining their lives like his older brother had, then he would gladly give his body a beating every day of the week.

Heath stared up at the ceiling and sighed. Hunter had fallen into the wrong crowd before they'd even moved to Chapel Cove, and he hadn't stopped running on the wild side since. Mom leaving Dad…leaving them…had hit the family hard, but Hunter acted out his rage by rebelling. And his delinquent ways had already cost him two terms in jail.

Would his big brother ever change?

Shrill tones from his cell phone had Heath bolting upright. He reached for the device on the counter beside his bed, then glanced at the caller ID. Pastor Keller, his boss or co-worker or fellow servant at Chapel Cove Community Church. However one labelled their relationship, the senior pastor had been one of Heath's closest friends.

"Don, what's up?" Trying to sound upbeat, Heath did his best to mask the fact that he was under strain today. The past two weeks visiting Hunter in prison had been exhausting—more mentally than physically—although those teens had expended his body today about as much as the trip to Hunter had tired his mind.

"Hi, Heath, hope I'm not disturbing you."

"Not at all."

"Listen, I know you've just returned from California, but I was wondering if you could do a short update tomorrow morning in church about your work with the youth?"

"Sure. That won't be a problem." It was easy to speak about one's passion—no prep needed.

"Great! Well, I'll see you tomorrow then."

"Yep. See you in the morning."

Heath cut the call and flopped back into the pillow, phone still firmly clasped between his fingers. He stared at the decade-old photo on his screen—the last image taken of him and his two brothers, two years before Hunter was arrested. At least their little brother, Hudson, had made something of his life. But then, he'd been afforded better opportunities than either Heath or Hunter. Maybe if they'd received football scholarships, they could've gone to college and become somebody.

Heath closed his eyes. He couldn't complain though. Thanks to

Uncle Trafford, he'd managed to go to Bible college at the age of twenty-five, taking up his first youth pastorate in Portland before he was thirty. He'd had eight wonderful years working with inner-city youths until he relocated back to Chapel Cove after his uncle fell ill. Fortunately, the position of youth pastor had opened up at the same time. Definitely a God-thing that he'd come home and been able to care for Uncle Trafford during his last few months.

Opening his mouth, Heath yawned widely. He dropped his phone on the bed and grabbed the spare pillow. Rolling over onto his side, he hugged it to his chest and released a contented sigh. Maybe he should just go to sleep now and hasten tomorrow's arrival. He couldn't wait for the morning service. It was crazy how much he missed the people from Chapel Cove Community Church, even though he'd only been away two Sundays. But ministers—especially those working with teens—needed a vacation too. Not that driving all the way to Los Angeles to visit his brother in prison was much of a rest. In fact, it was trying and tiring. It had been so much easier to see Hunter during his first term in jail. Portland was only a ninety-minute commute. But his second arrest had happened in LA, and California was so much farther away from home. Consequently, he only got to visit Hunter once a year.

His chest tightened. Would he have ended up like his older brother if God hadn't saved him? With a drunk for a father, it was entirely likely. And a definite yes if Reese had pressed charges that night.

She'd been two months shy of the age of consent. Although regretting their actions, Reese had said the blame was not his alone to bear—she'd known exactly what she was doing when she stepped into this camper after that Valentine's date.

Heath regretted his mistake every day, but thanked God often for Uncle Trafford's influence on his life.

In a few months, Hunter would come up for parole. Heath had

given him a lot to think about after he'd said goodbye on Thursday. If God was merciful and Hunter got out early, hopefully his brother would turn his life around.

As he had done.

"Three strikes and you're out," Heath warned before leaving. He hated the thought, but another arrest could see Hunter behind bars for fifteen years to life. All Heath could do now was pray earnestly that *this* time his sharing of the gospel would fall on fertile soil. So far, all he'd done was sow seeds on the path, the fowls of the air snatching the seed before it had time to root. Hunter had never shown the slightest interest in spiritual things. This time, though, things somehow seemed different. Hunter had asked questions and even asked Heath to keep praying for him, not to give up on him.

Heath yawned again, the long drive back from LA taking its toll. Perhaps he'd close his eyes awhile before grabbing his camera and going for a stroll to photograph yet another incredible Oregon sunset.

CHAPTER THREE

REESE PAUSED for the umpteenth time in the forty minutes she'd been jogging. Bending over, she pressed her palms to her knees and panted, trying to catch her breath. Her chest burned and her legs shook as if every muscle protested the harsh treatment. How had she become this unfit in such a short time? Perhaps she'd pushed herself too hard on this run in her efforts to make up for lost time.

She'd first jogged out to the lavender farm and back. Until way past her teen years, there'd been a view of the rolling purple fields from her bedroom window. Now, newer developments blotted out the panoramic landscape. Up close though, the farm was just as beautiful as she'd remembered.

Blowing out a breath, Reese straightened. Not ready to return to the four walls that had caged her these past few weeks, she continued to weave her way through the streets of Chapel Cove, past the schools she'd attended—kindergarten, grade school, junior high, and high school. Oh the memories each stirred. Some bitter. Some sweet. And some, just bittersweet.

Leaving the schools behind her, her thoughts churning, Reese jogged to the town park and around its perimeter, pausing now and then to rest on a bench. For a brief moment, she considered returning home—perhaps she'd punished her body enough for its wayward spell—but she still wanted to head to the beach and fill her lungs with the smell of sea air. What was a few more miles, anyway? Her body couldn't ache more than it already did.

Reese's route took her past the cemetery and the outskirts of the central shopping area on Main Street. As she neared the jetty beside the amusement park, the brightly colored Ferris wheel filled her view. Young and old milled about the park and the boardwalk, enjoying the last hours the Saturday afternoon had to offer.

Taking slow steps, Reese strolled down the jetty to the farthest point. Above her, cawing seagulls floated on the breeze, the nostalgic sound reminiscent of carefree days spent with her friends along these shores. Dark clouds had rolled in, and Reese prayed she'd make it home before the storm broke.

Turning around, her eyes scanned the shoreline. Her heart thudded against her ribs then constricted. No way. Surely that wasn't Heath Brock's camper still planted firmly on the same site in the RV park? But then why wouldn't it be? The camper belonged to his uncle, and his uncle owned the park. Chances that Heath still lived there though were slim to none. Surely, by now, he must've moved on?

Like a siren's song, the camper drew Reese back across the jetty and down the beach, closer and closer. She paused to pick up a shell, admiring its beauty as she slowly put one foot in front of the other. Despite the ominous clouds rolling closer, she couldn't stop herself from moving toward the humble home she'd vowed never to return to. Because if she had, she would've given up on her dreams.

For all the good her achievements had done her. Over two decades and she'd come almost full circle, having little more to show now than when she'd left Chapel Cove—besides her face plastered on dated magazines. Soon, the fashion world would forget all about Reese Aylward, if it hadn't already.

Tucking the shell in her pocket, Reese paused, taking in the sight before her. Apart from the surrounding trees being way taller than when she was eighteen—well, almost eighteen—and the camper looking a little more weathered, everything looked the same as when she'd run from there in the early hours of that morning so long ago.

As she stood staring, memories of her and Heath's one night of passion, their one big mistake, flooded over her.

Suddenly, the door clicked open and a man stepped out, camera dangling around his neck. He looked up and his eyes widened.

Couldn't be…

Heath.

Reese's heart thudded to a stop. Whoa, he still looked as good as he had at twenty-one. If not better. That youth pastor had better be even better looking.

No way. It couldn't be. Was the apparition standing merely a few feet away from his camper really Reese? Besides the glossy magazine covers and television ads, Heath hadn't seen Reese in almost twenty-two years.

She looked weary. Older. Then again, she wasn't made up for the cameras.

Instinctively his hand clasped the 35mm hanging around his neck. Memories of the day on the beach when he'd taken the photos for her portfolio flashed through his mind. How had they slid from friends' zone for almost five years to lovers overnight? Well, for one unforgettable night.

Heat crept up the back of his neck. He sucked in a breath and lowered his voice. "Helloooo, Clarise."

Seriously? After all this time the first thing he says to the girl he's been in love with almost his entire life is something so juvenile?

Like a rabbit caught in a car's headlights, Reese remained frozen. Then she glanced back over her shoulder, and Heath wondered if she'd bolt. She'd done it before, and he hadn't heard from her again.

Feelings he'd never been able to bury stirred. He yearned to take her in his arms.

No! No he didn't. Those thoughts were improper. She was a married woman, that much he did know. And he was a man of the cloth.

Her mouth opened. "H–Heath? Is that really you? Oh my, it's been what…"

"Twenty-two years." But who was counting?

He strode toward her. "You look…great." Although the light didn't sparkle in her eyes as it once had. Had life treated her badly? From what he'd seen, it hadn't seemed so.

She shrugged. "Oh, it's Reese. Remember I ditched the 'Cla' a long, long time ago." She managed a weak smile.

"Well then, best I start over. Helloooo, Reese." Cracking a grin, he shook his head. "Doesn't have quite the same ring to it, does it? How am I to tease you now?"

Reese lifted her hand and twirled her ponytail around her fingers. "Oh, I think we passed the teasing phase a lifetime ago."

She lowered her gaze and kicked at the sand with her shoes before venturing a glance at him again. "I–I should go. The storm's coming closer, and I'd hate to get wet on my run home. Last thing I need is the flu."

She turned then paused to peer over her shoulder once more, this time at him. "It was nice to see you again, Heath."

Reese had barely taken a few steps when Heath felt a raindrop pelt his cheek.

"Wait." He jogged toward her. "I think you're too late. Let me drive you, or you'll be soaked by the time you reach your house. Unless, of course, you're staying in the RV park too." Which he seriously doubted.

More drops fell, fast and furiously.

Reese glanced at the dark skies and falling rain, then back at Heath. She nodded.

"Great. I'll grab my keys." Heath dashed for the camper. Feet still planted on the beach sand, he leaned inside and snatched his pickup's keys from the small counter above the mini fridge. Shutting the door of the camper, he swung around, slam-bang into Reese. He hadn't realized she'd followed him and stood so close behind him.

Instinctively, his arms wrapped around Reese to steady her.

She quickly jerked away.

An ache formed in his chest. If only she'd pulled away so easily that Valentine's night. Maybe they might've still been together.

Maybe, but probably not. She'd had big dreams to follow. And a small town loser would only have hampered those dreams. Not that she'd said as much, but she had to have thought it many times.

"Truck's on the other side of the camper." Heath led the way to his red '89 Dodge Ram. He opened the door and Reese slid onto the seat.

After slamming the door shut—didn't close any other way—he

hurried to the driver's side and clambered behind the wheel. Heath turned to Reese, too nervous to smile. "Where to?"

"My parents' house. Same old place. You know where that is?"

He nodded. Although he'd never been inside the house where Reese had grown up, he'd always known where she lived. And he knew her parents from church, although they had no idea that he and their daughter had history.

The drive to Pioneer Lane was silent. Reese offered nothing in the way of conversation as she stared out of the passenger window. Even though Heath longed to ask her a million questions like what she was doing back in Chapel Cove, how long she would be staying, and was she still married—yes, he'd noticed her fingers bore no wedding rings and a flicker of hope had ignited at the implication—he remained mute. Best not to venture where he shouldn't. Likely she was visiting her parents for her upcoming birthday, she'd taken off her wedding rings for her run, and soon she'd jet out of Chapel Cove again, back to New York and her rich husband.

He pulled the truck to a stop outside number twenty-five and cracked his door open.

"Oh, don't get out. I can open the door myself," Reese said, shooting him a glance. The door clicked as she yanked on the handle. Then she turned to look at him once more, her gaze lingering this time. "Thanks for saving me from a soaking. It was…good to see you again. Really good."

She slid from the car, and Heath couldn't help wondering if he had just let her slide out of his life too.

Again.

Soaking her aching muscles in a hot, bubble bath, Reese closed her eyes and slipped lower until the water covered her to her neck. Ah, so good.

She breathed the scent of lavender in deeply, hoping the calming herb would ease away the anxiety overwhelming her since seeing Heath. As if it wasn't enough to deal with her feelings of inadequacy over her failed marriage and career. Now she had to process all the emotions that seeing her old love, her first love, had stirred. She was so confused. Surely she couldn't still feel something for him? After all this time?

But why then had her heart beat faster just being near him? Why had she clammed up like a schoolgirl on the ride home? And why, oh why, couldn't she get him out of her mind?

She needed a distraction. And she knew exactly what. Or who.

After a long soak, Reese stepped out of the bath. After drying herself, she wrapped a towel around her wet hair then donned her pajamas. It wasn't unusual for her to be clad in them before dinner. Heck, some days she'd just plain never gotten out of the nightclothes.

Reese pattered down the staircase, following the aroma of her mother's cooking. With a smile curving her lips, she burst into the kitchen and sniffed the air. "Something smells divine."

Stooped low, peering into the oven, Mom glanced over her shoulder and grinned. She straightened and wiped her hands on her floral apron. "My famous lasagne. Only a few more minutes and we can eat. Just waiting for the cheese to brown slightly. Do you want to call your father? I think he's reading the newspaper in the living room—at least, he was the last time I saw him."

"Sure, Mom." Reese whipped around and bounced back toward the door.

"Reese," Mom called after her.

Fingers wrapped around the door handle, Reese paused and turned. "Uh-huh?"

"You're in good spirits this evening. Seems the run did you good."

"It was...ah...life changing." Thankfully the bath had balanced the effects of that run in more ways than just her sore legs. Maybe this was exactly the nudge she'd needed to put herself back out there. Who would've thought it would be her first love, and not her last, that would make her jump back into the dating pool?

Flashing another smile at her mother, Reese left the kitchen. She hurried to the living room to call her father. She couldn't wait to sink her teeth into all that melted cheese and pasta. The exercise had left her famished. Only once they'd eaten and she was about to head to bed would she tell her folks about her decision to join them for the morning church service, otherwise Mom would spend the entire dinner gushing on about the youth pastor. Hopefully he was as handsome and wonderful as her mother claimed—she needed a serious distraction from Heath Brock.

And to tide her over between bed time and slumber and keep her thoughts from a certain beach bum, she'd call Kristina. Time to let her friend know she was back and what was happening in her life. Kristina was bound to be at church tomorrow, so it would be best not to shock her with a sudden appearance. Besides, Kristina would want to know everything that was going on, and if she was to make a good first impression on Mr. Youth Pastor, having her best friend hanging around asking questions about her sudden divorce and career suicide wasn't a good idea. Getting it all out in the open tonight was her only option.

But she'd have to put off calling Nai until tomorrow afternoon. No doubt Kristina would keep her on the phone until she fell asleep. She just hoped she woke up in time to get ready for the service.

CHAPTER FOUR

REESE'S MOM pointed to the familiar pew on her right, somewhere about the middle of the church. Her parents were such creatures of habit, they had claimed that same row ever since Reese could remember.

Reese shuffled between the pews, leaving the first two places open for Mom and Dad, then eased down onto the cushioned seat.

Mom followed, then Dad. As they sat, they closed their eyes and bowed their heads in prayer.

Reese's gaze skittered around the hallowed space and memories flooded her mind of all the Sundays she, Nai, and Kristina had spent in this building, on these same butt-numbing benches. Except, she didn't think her behind would ache today. The pews, the same wooden ones, were now upholstered and padded—both the seat and the backrest. A pleasant change since she'd last been inside these four walls. How long ago had that been…five, six years?

She raised her eyes to the paneled A-frame roof with its steep pitch. It had always reminded her of the hull of a capsized boat.

Her gaze drifted to the large cross behind the pulpit and the two long and narrow windows on either side. Another new feature, the clear glass had been replaced with beautiful stained glass works of art—the nativity on the left, and the ascension on the right. Those stories had fascinated her so as a child. Why, oh why, had that fascination for Jesus waned when she hit fame and fortune? Had God allowed her to lose everything to bring her back to a place of dependence, of dedication to him?

Uncomfortable at the reminder of how her life had turned out, she glanced away from the windows and the cross. Only then did she spot the familiar gray head with its perfect hairdo four rows up ahead.

Nai's Aunt Ivy!

Oh, the three girls had spent so many wonderful hours in Aunt Ivy's bookshop just behind Chapel Cove's main street. First thing after the service she would go and greet her.

With that, Aunt Ivy turned and grinned at the person sitting behind her, a little to her right. The person, hidden by the congregants in the two rows separating him or her from Reese, leaned forward and Reese's heart lurched.

Heath.

Would there be no getting away from him now that they'd bumped into each other?

Reese slid lower in the seat, not that it would help at all to hide her from Heath if he should turn around now. He was bound to spot her. If she could see him, he most certainly would be able to see her.

Please, please, Lord, keep him looking to the front.

It was the first prayer she'd shot to heaven in a very long time. She hadn't even prayed for God to save her marriage. She'd given up on her life with Lloyd way before it finally ended.

Okay, maybe she had prayed to get a decent price for her rings. And well, that prayer hadn't been answered had it?

After a short exchange of words, Heath nodded and slowly eased back. Before he disappeared from Reese's line of vision, he looked over his shoulder.

Right into Reese's gaze.

Great! Yet another unanswered prayer.

Mouth widening into a grin, Heath tipped his head in greeting.

Reese quickly glanced away, pretending she hadn't seen. Right...as if he wouldn't know with the brief eye-lock neither of them had been able to escape.

Hopefully her mom would introduce her to that youth pastor as soon as possible after the service.

Music began to fill the sanctuary and Heath shifted his attention to the front of the church as Aiden McConnell, the worship leader, stepped up to the microphone. Aiden had been one of the first changes Heath had slowly introduced at the church. At first, Aiden and his team only played once every few weeks, but it wasn't long before the church members were asking if he could lead worship more often. Way, way more often. Soon the organist gracefully bowed out, grateful for the opportunity to retire from playing the hymns at every service, something she'd been praying about for a while. The rejuvenated worship led by the now thirty-year-old musician was the best thing to happen to the church Pastor Don had confided to Heath, and over the past four years, the church had seen good growth, particularly with a surge of young people joining Chapel Cove Community Church.

As Aiden began to sing the words to "Oceans", Heath's favorite worship song, Heath closed his eyes and raised his hands toward heaven. Focusing his thoughts on God would shift them away from Reese. He hadn't been able to get her out of his mind since bumping into her yesterday afternoon.

Forgive me, Father, for where my thoughts have been stuck these past couple of hours. Reese was a married woman. She'd never be his. And he shouldn't be thinking about her. It was wrong. It was sin.

His eyes burned with tears that escaped and trailed his cheeks. *Forgive me, Lord.*

The sooner Reese returned home to city life, the better.

At the sound of a thud nearby, then a gasp from one of the congregation, a shriek from another, Heath's eyes shot open to the empty seat where Ivy Macnamara had been sitting merely minutes ago. The music came to a sudden halt. Swiping at his cheeks, Heath turned to see Ivy lying crumpled in the aisle on the blue carpet.

"Someone call 911!" He flew out of his seat and vaulted past the three young people from his youth group seated beside him, panic etched on their faces. Adrenaline pumping, Heath fell to his knees beside Ivy and rolled her over onto her back. He touched her cheek. Her skin was cold and clammy.

Heath shook her by the shoulders. "Ivy! Ivy!" Getting no response, he leaned close to her pallid face and listened for a few painstaking seconds. Dread dug its talons into his heart and tightened its grip. She wasn't breathing.

Feeling the congregation press in around them, Heath bellowed, "Please, people, return to your seats and give me room to work. Instead of standing and staring, go pray!"

The words were barely out before he regretted his tone. But he couldn't concern himself about that now. He had to try and save Ivy's life.

Heath glanced at a few congregants, his gaze entreating. "I–it's what Ivy needs most right now." As he snapped his attention back to Ivy and placed the heel of one hand in the center of her chest, the other hand on top of that, a shuffle sounded around him and the voice of Pastor Don asked everyone to please return to their seats and pray for the situation.

Good. Breathing room.

The worship team began to softly play once again.

Locking his elbows, he leaned forward and compressed Ivy's chest about two inches. Remembering to do the new method of continuous CPR without mouth-to-mouth breathing recommended for non-medical people because it was easier, he pumped at a hundred compressions per minute. All the while, the disco song "Staying Alive" resounded in his mind—a neat little trick he'd been taught to keep the beat—his focus on nothing and no one but the dying woman beside him.

Only when someone sobbed from the other side of Ivy and took her hand, did Heath glance up. Reese knelt beside the prostrate woman, tears trickling down her cheeks and smudging her mascara.

Suddenly, another person groaned as they eased down onto their knees beside Reese.

Heath looked up into the worried eyes of Dr. Jeff Johnson and asked, "Heart attack?"

Concern creased the doctor's face, more so than one would expect. This woman was no ordinary patient to the good doctor.

"Probably." Dr. Johnson shifted his gaze to stare at Ivy. Then he whirled around to Reese and dropped a set of keys into her hand. "Be a honey and get my medical bag from my car so that I can assist Heath. Please. It's the black sedan right outside on the left."

Reese stared at the doctor, eyes wide.

"Go!" Heath shouted, annoyance grating his frayed nerves. Sheesh, was the woman too high and mighty to do an errand for someone in desperate need of help?

Reese scurried to her feet and fled down the aisle, high-heeled boots and all.

"Did someone call 911?" Heath bellowed, his tone not quite as sharp as the first time he'd addressed the congregants.

"I did," a voice shouted from behind him.

By the time Reese returned, Dr. Johnson had taken over the chest compressions from Heath to give him a short break.

Heath wiped the sweat from his brow once more with the sleeve of his shirt before taking over from Dr. Johnson. Now the good doctor could use his bag of magic tricks to help keep Ivy alive until the paramedics arrived.

Dr. Johnson dove into his bag and retrieved a packaged item.

"What's that?" Reese asked.

"Bag valve mask. Or BVM," Dr. Johnson replied. "Easier to give her oxygen this way."

With skilled hands, he quickly assembled the mask then pressed it firmly around Ivy's nose and mouth. He squeezed the bag and began counting, "One one thousand, two one thousand, three one thousand, four one thousand, five one thousand, six one thousand." He squeezed the bag again. "One. One one thousand, two ..."

Realizing the doctor had his hands full with the BVM, and unsure whether he could keep up the compressions effectively until the EMTs arrived, Heath panted, "Anyone else ...know how to do CPR?"

Only silence responded.

Great. Already his arm muscles ached. Felt as if he was lifting two hundred pound weights in the gym. How much longer could he keep doing this?

Despite the exhaustion, as long as was necessary.

In the distance, a siren squealed, and Heath's spirits lifted. Not much longer, thank You, Lord. It had been at least four or five minutes since Ivy had collapsed—a fair amount of time for one person to be doing constant chest compressions, except for the very short break when Dr. Johnson had spelled him.

Moments after the siren wailed to a stop outside the church, two EMTs burst through the doors, pushing a gurney. Parking the moveable stretcher in the aisle, Riley Jordan and Pete Bennet rushed to Ivy and set their equipment down beside her.

"Riley...Pete...am I happy to see you!" Dr. Johnson exclaimed as the EMTs knelt.

Pete waved off Heath and resumed the chest compressions.

Relieved, Heath shoved to his feet and moved back to give the crew more space to work.

Stepping beside Heath, Reese's moist eyes searched his. She looked so afraid that he longed to wrap her in his arms and tell her that her best friend's aunt would be okay. But he couldn't do that. Reese was married, he was the youth pastor, and he had no assurance that Ivy would make it through.

"What do we have here?" Riley, the senior EMT asked as he sliced Ivy's blouse open with a pair of scissors. Ivy wouldn't be happy about that—he'd heard her mention it was her favorite blouse.

"It's Ivy Macnamara," Dr. Johnson said. "She collapsed in the aisle little more than five minutes ago. I suspect she's suffered a heart attack. She's still not breathing."

Offering a small nod, Riley began attaching defibrillator pads to Ivy's chest.

Riley and Pete would need some background info on what happened. Heath should tell them the little he knew. "I was seated behind her in the service. Shortly before she collapsed, Ivy turned to me and said she was feeling a little strange, that she'd had indigestion for a couple days." They didn't need to know she'd actually joked with him, asking him to catch her if she passed out.

Riley offered a quick nod then barked, "Please step farther back."

Heath and Reese took a few steps away from them.

Riley's gaze landed on Dr. Johnson. "Would you continue to bag her between shocks?"

"Of course."

Riley took over the CPR from Pete as he, Pete, and Dr. Johnson fixed their eyes on the defibrillator's screen, watching for a shockable rhythm.

A wild, squiggly line shot up and down the screen, and Dr. Johnson shouted, "VF! Thank You, Lord!"

Immediately, Pete set the voltage and changed the defibrillator reading to "Shock". The machine buzzed, indicating it was ready.

Dr. Johnson hurriedly lifted the mask from Ivy's face, and he and Riley backed away as Pete pressed the shock button.

Ivy's body jerked as electric currents shot through her chest to her heart.

After Pete adjusted the defibrillator, turning off shock mode, Riley quickly picked up the compressions while Dr. Johnson placed the BVM over Ivy's nose and mouth and squeezed oxygen into her lungs.

Two minutes later the three medical men repeated the process as the defibrillator delivered another shock to Ivy's heart.

Ivy gasped then groaned. Her eyes flickered open briefly before sliding shut again.

Heath breathed a sigh of relief as his gaze shot to the screen. A regular spiked pattern... Thank you, Jesus. Even though beating fast, her heart rhythm seemed more normal.

Riley rolled Ivy into the recovery position. "Ivy, can you hear me?"

Ivy's head moved up and down ever so slightly.

"I'm EMT Riley Jordan. You collapsed in church. We suspect you've suffered a heart attack."

Once Pete had attached the BVM to an oxygen supply, he set up an IV line and pumped meds into Ivy's body.

Dr. Johnson leaned in closer. "Just rest, Ivy. You're going to be all right. You're in good hands, and I won't let anything happen to you."

He turned to the EMTs. "She'll need to be medevacked by air to Portland. It's the nearest cardiac unit. I have a colleague at the Portland Heart and Vascular Institute—a cardiologist. I'll contact him and see if he's available to take over Ivy's treatment the moment she arrives."

A colleague? And a heart specialist to boot. Only God's grace.

Dr. Johnson continued, "In the meantime, take Ivy to the clinic—I'll treat her there while we wait for the helicopter." He huffed out a sigh and muttered, "It's times like this when I wish the town had a proper hospital, not just a health clinic."

Hating the thought of her arriving in Portland alone, Heath asked, "C–can I go with her?" Ivy had become like the mother he'd never had.

Dr. Johnson shook his head. "I'm afraid there's no room for passengers." He rose from where he'd knelt beside Ivy and squeezed Heath's shoulder. "Don't worry. I know what she means to you, but she'll be in good hands."

"I know, Doc. And you'll be with her in the helicopter."

"Oh no. Unfortunately not. Like I said, there's no room for passengers. I'll drive up once the helicopter's safely in the air."

No. Dr. Johnson shouldn't drive all that way on those windy mountain roads on his own. "I'll take you," Heath said. He'd planned to drive anyway. He'd just wait a while so the doc could go with.

The EMTs moved Ivy to the gurney, talking to her all the time. With speed, they wheeled her down the aisle.

"I'd appreciate that. I'll see you at the clinic then." Dr. Johnson grabbed his bag. He paused and swung back to Heath. His eyes moistened, and in a gruff voice he choked out, "And thank you, Heath. Your quick response might just have saved Ivy's life."

The doctor pivoted and hurried down the aisle.

As Heath started to follow, Reese stepped in front of him. "Where are you going?"

"To the clinic, then Portland." He tried to ease past her.

Reese gripped his arm. "Take me with you. Please."

Having Reese as company might not be the greatest idea, but she seemed desperate to go.

One look into those pleading puppy dog eyes and all Heath's common sense crumbled. He nodded.

Reese's downturned mouth curved upward. "Great! Let me grab my bag and Aunt Ivy's. I'll meet you outside."

Reese snatched Aunt Ivy's handbag from the pew where the elderly woman had sat not fifteen minutes ago, although it felt like a lifetime since Nai's aunt had turned to smile at Heath.

Heads bowed, her parents were still in earnest prayer.

Leaning forward, Reese touched her father's shoulder. He opened his eyes and Reese whispered, "They're taking Aunt Ivy to Portland. I'm driving there with Heath."

Mom's eyes fluttered open too. "What's that, Reese?"

"I said, they're taking Aunt Ivy to Portland. I'm driving there with Heath." Reese had raised her voice a little so that her mom could hear.

Surprise registered on her mother's face before Mom smiled and nodded. "Take care, sweetheart. We'll continue to pray for Ivy."

"Thanks, Mom. Oh, would you mind passing my handbag? It's on the floor beneath my seat."

Mom complied with another smile.

Reese had almost reached the front door when someone grabbed her by the arm. She turned to see who had slowed her pace.

"Kristina!" Reese flung her arms around her friend, overjoyed to see her. She so needed a hug from someone.

"What happened?" Still holding Reese's hand, Kristina eased out of the embrace. "I couldn't see from the back row."

"Oh, Kris, it's too awful. Poor Aunt Ivy."

Kristina's brown, doe-like eyes widened, and she gasped. "Aunt Ivy?"

"Yes. She suffered a heart attack."

Kristina covered her mouth with her hand, concern filling her eyes. "Oh no!"

Only then did Reese notice Kristina's twin brother, Roman, hobbling toward them on crutches. Kristina had told Reese on the phone last night about his accident.

Roman wrapped his arms around Reese, the crutches banging against her calves. "Reese, look at you! As beautiful as ever. How long has it been, girl?" He leaned back and held her gaze.

Still the charmer. And he did look good. No longer the gangly teenager she'd grown up with, Roman was handsome, muscular, tanned. If trying to date the youth pastor didn't work out, Reese could always steer her attentions Roman's way to get her mind off Heath Brock.

She swallowed hard. *Please, stop staring at me with those chocolatey eyes.*

"Twenty years at least, I'm sure." Taking a step away from

Roman, Reese shifted her attention to Kristina. "I'm sorry but I have to run. They're transferring Aunt Ivy to Portland by medevac. I'm driving there with Heath. We'll catch up another time, okay?" Reese turned to go.

Kristina grabbed her arm for the second time in minutes. "Heath? As in *your* Heath?"

Reese blew out an exasperated breath. "There is no *my* Heath, but yes, *that* Heath."

Kristina's mouth curved into a smile. She gave Reese's arm a squeeze before releasing her hold. "Well, well, God sure does work in mysterious ways."

"I–I have to go." Reese whirled around and fled from the church.

Outside, Heath pulled his truck to a stop.

Reese slid onto the gray leather bench seat. Already the ambulance had made a right turn out of the church grounds, lights flashing and sirens blaring. She fastened her seat belt then leaned against the door, maximizing the distance between her and Heath. As if the seat wasn't already wide enough.

"That was fast. Were you here in your truck?"

Heath nodded. "Thankfully."

"But your place is a stone's throw away. I would've figured you'd walk to church."

"Usually I do, but I had plans for right after the service, so I drove."

"Oh... Do you need to call someone to cancel?" A familiar feeling twisted her gut. Ridiculous. She couldn't be jealous. Could she?

"Nope. Just plans of my own."

Reese could do nothing to stop the sense of relief that washed over her.

The drive to the clinic was quiet, Heath's strong jaw set as he focused on following the ambulance and Dr. Johnson's car up North Wharf Road. Clearly, Ivy's heart attack had upset him.

Rapping his thumbs against the steering wheel, Heath drew in a deep breath then cleared his throat before glancing at Reese. "Um, I'm sorry I snapped at you."

He looked genuinely sorry. But for what?

Reese brushed a piece of fluff from her black leggings, glancing at him from the corner of her eye. "What are you talking about? You didn't snap at me."

"Not now. Back at the church when Dr. Johnson asked you to get his bag from the car."

Oh, that. She'd already forgotten about it.

"It's all right. Everyone's nerves were on edge in those moments so totally understandable."

Heath shifted on his seat. "I–it's just, I was fearful for Ivy. She's sort of become like the mother I never had. Might've been my aunt too, had Uncle Trafford lived. I think they were quite keen on each other.

"Speaking of aunts, you should let Nai know what's happened."

Oh goodness, she should. Unless Kristina had already done so. But with Kristina needing to drive her brother around, it's likely she wouldn't have time to call Nai until she got home.

"I will. Soon as we get to the clinic." Reese glanced out of the window pondering a question for Heath. She might as well ask. Decided, she turned and faced him. "So, where did you learn to do that?"

Heath's brow wrinkled with a frown. "Do what?"

"CPR. Save someone's life." She hated to admit it, but she was pretty impressed.

"Well, only time will tell whether my efforts managed to save Ivy."

Reese reached out and placed her hand lightly on his arm.

"Don't. Don't even think that. She's going to be okay, and it's all because of your quick thinking."

Suddenly aware that her thumb caressed his skin, she withdrew her hand, her heart beating wildly.

Heath's lips pursed. Was he disappointed that she'd cut short the brief touch, or annoyed that she'd even ventured into familiar territory?

Dipping his head in a slight nod, Heath said, "You're right, of course. But it'll be because of the power of prayer and God's grace if Ivy makes it—not because of anything I've done."

Good grief, the man was certainly humble. And seemingly religious. She'd never seen that side of him before. He must've found God in all the years they'd been apart.

As for herself, she'd lost touch with the Almighty.

Reese filled her lungs then exhaled slowly. "So, the CPR... Why? How? Did you become some superhero or fireman while I was away from Chapel Cove?"

A belly laugh burst from Heath's mouth, and he glanced at her. She'd forgotten how attractive his deep laugh was. And how his green eyes lit up when he smiled.

He shook his head. "Nothing like that."

Reese feigned disappointment. "So then, something like what?"

Outside, the sirens wailed to a stop as the ambulance pulled up outside the clinic, Dr. Johnson right behind them. Slowing the pickup, Heath turned into the parking lot and stopped a little way from the ambulance. He cut the engine then turned to Reese, arm stretching out on the backrest.

"When I was working with the inner city youth in Portland some years ago, I soon came to realize that learning basic first aid and CPR would be a very handy skill to have working with troubled kids. This isn't the first time I've proven that right."

Youth work?

Like headlights shining through the fog, realization dawned. "Wait... A–are *you* the youth pastor at Chapel Cove Community Church?"

"You didn't know?"

How would she?

Well there went using the youth pastor to take her mind off Heath. And as tempting a distraction as Roman would be, Kristina would never forgive her for using her brother like that.

Reese reached into her jacket pocket for her phone. Pressing her finger on the contacts icon, she pulled up Nai's number, hesitating before dialing.

"I–I should call Nai. She needs to be told about Aunt Ivy."

CHAPTER FIVE

WHILE THEY waited inside the clinic for the helicopter to land over the road at the fire station, Reese filled Nai in on Ivy's situation. Nai said she'd be on the first plane out of Austin. It would be several hours before she arrived in Portland. Still, Reese decided it would be better to fill Nai in about her divorce when she saw her and explain why she was back in Chapel Cove.

Heath sat a few seats down from Reese, head bowed in his hands.

Reese eyed him out the corner of her eye. She couldn't believe *he* was the youth pastor her mother had raved about. What were the odds? But with her luck with men, it shouldn't have surprised her.

She looked through the window toward the fire station. Where was that helicopter? As soon as it landed, they could be on their way to Portland with the good doctor. Thankfully they'd have someone else in the car and she wouldn't be alone with Heath.

Just then, Dr. Johnson appeared. He called to Heath. "Sorry to have kept you waiting. There's been a change of plans."

Heath rose, hooking his thumbs in his pants pockets. "Oh. What's changed?"

"There were no available helicopters, so they're sending a turbo-prop plane instead," Dr. Johnson explained. "As such, I'll be able to fly with Ivy—there'll be space. We're transporting her now by ambulance to the airfield."

Heath patted Dr. Johnson's shoulder. "God is good. I'm glad you can be with her, Doc. I know you'll take good care of Ivy."

"Oh, that I will," Dr. Johnson said.

Heath turned to go then stopped. "So, Doc, if you're leaving town, who'll be on call for medical emergencies? You never leave without having someone cover for you, and this is way too unexpected to have a replacement planned."

A smile twitched at one corner of the doctor's mouth. "I've a doctor joining the clinic. He arrived yesterday. I'll just let him know he has to start a day earlier."

Heath frowned. "You're handing over the welfare of the town to a total stranger?"

Dr. Johnson's amusement morphed into a full-blown grin. "The town's in good hands, Heath. You'll like the guy. I promise." Dr. Johnson whirled around and walked away as fast as his aging legs could carry him. "I'll see you in Portland," he shouted over his shoulder.

Heath glanced at Reese then back at Dr. Johnson's retreating form. "It's just as well he's appointed someone to assist him. The town's growing, and Dr. Johnson isn't getting any younger."

Heath tipped his head toward the door. "I guess we can be on our way then."

As they fastened their seatbelts in the truck, Reese asked, "Is there something between Aunt Ivy and the doc? He seems quite taken with her."

Heath merely shrugged.

Soon they drove past the cemetery. Hopefully a place they wouldn't visit any time soon. Reese pressed her eyes together. *Please, God. You have to save Ivy.*

Once Heath had passed the town limits, he accelerated and cruised down the open road.

Mumbling something to Heath about being exhausted and taking a short nap, Reese curled up against the door and closed her eyes.

When she woke, Heath had just pulled his truck to a stop.

"We're here? Already?" It felt as if she'd only just closed her eyes.

"Yup."

She stared at the two-story building ahead, a feeling of angst descending over her like the ominous clouds of yesterday. She shot Heath another glance. By the look on his face, he was feeling the same way too.

"What time is it?" Stretching, she released a yawn, quickly covering her mouth with her hand.

"Nearly eleven-thirty."

Almost lunch time. No wonder her stomach felt hollow. It had been a while since breakfast. So long as it didn't groan, she could live with the emptiness for a little longer. Once they got an update on Aunt Ivy, however, they should probably find somewhere to eat. Hopefully this hospital had a coffee shop. Most did.

They exited the truck and walked toward the large glass doors of Portland Heart and Vascular Institute.

The hospital's interior was pristine. Glossed tiled floors, some plush couches and chairs near the reception, and yes!—a coffee shop.

"Let's find out about Ivy, then we can grab a cup," Heath said. "Maybe a bite to eat."

Had the excitement of seeing a place where they could get food shown that much on her face?

Just then, someone called Heath's name. Seemed to come from the coffee shop.

Heath turned, then pointed and waved. "It's Dr. Johnson. Come, let's find out what he knows." He took her lightly by the elbow and steered her toward the coffee shop.

Dr. Johnson rose and gave Heath a bear hug. "You made it."

Heath grinned. "We did. I take it Ivy has been admitted?"

The doctor nodded as they sat. "She went into surgery about forty-five minutes ago."

Reese sucked in a sharp breath. "Surgery? Oh no."

"I sent the 12-lead EKG reading to the cardiology team ahead of the flight, so they knew what to do when Ivy got here." Dr. Johnson folded his arms and rested them on the table. "Unfortunately, I'm no heart expert, just a hick country doctor, so I couldn't make a conclusive diagnosis, although I do suspect she had a blockage."

As the doctor spoke, he glanced in turn at Heath and Reese. "They're doing a coronary angioplasty and stent insertion which will open up the blocked blood vessels that supply the heart muscle."

Poor Aunt Ivy. Reese wished Nai was already there. Her friend was going to try and catch the early afternoon flight. Hopefully she'd be successful. It would be great to see her again, despite the circumstances.

Reese turned to Dr. Johnson and asked, "Is it major surgery?"

The doctor shook his head. "No. Depending on whether or not there are any complications, an hour or two max. It's quite a simple procedure actually, *if* the arteries are suitable for stenting."

"And if they aren't?" Heath worried his lip as he stared at Dr. Johnson.

Concern washed over the doctor's face. It was obvious that wasn't an option he wanted to entertain. The man cared for Aunt Ivy, that much was clear.

"T–then it could mean open heart s–surgery." Dr. Johnson's voice cracked, and he heaved a sigh.

Oh, dear God, no. Please, don't let that happen.

Heath rested a hand on the doctor's shoulder to console him. "Is your colleague performing the surgery?"

Dr. Johnson shook his head. "Unfortunately not. He's away on vacation in Europe, but when I called him, he assured me that all the surgeons at this facility are top class. So we've nothing to be concerned about." He looked at Reese, then Heath. "Right?"

"She's in God's hands—that's what's most important." Heath patted the man's shoulder before shoving to his feet.

"Coffee for everyone? Maybe a pastry? My treat."

Reese and the doctor both nodded.

Heath strode to the counter and placed their drinks order, along with three almond Danish pastries. Once the order had been filled, he returned to the table and set the tray down. Then he eased back into his chair and said grace.

Opening his eyes, Heath leaned closer to the elderly doctor. "Can I ask you something personal?"

Dr. Johnson reached for his coffee and snack, his peppery brows quirking. "Ask away. My life's an open book. Sort of. Except, of course, for anything that falls under doctor/patient confidentiality."

"Are you in love with Ivy?" Heath chuckled. "Or are matters of the heart doctor/patient confidential too?" His fingers wrapped around his disposable paper cup and he took a long drink.

Graying head bobbing up and down, Dr. Johnson smiled. "I am. And I fully intend to tell her the moment she's well enough to listen to me. W–what happened this morning…well, that made me realize it's way past time Ivy knew how I felt. I've left it far too long. But I knew that she and your uncle were keen on each other, and I wanted to give her enough time to get over him."

A grin widened across Heath's face, showing his approval. "Uncle Trafford has been gone for five years. I think maybe you've just been a little chicken to be vulnerable?" He cocked his head and began to make a clucking sound.

Dr. Johnson chuckled softly and nodded. "I guess I have." He lifted the Danish and took a healthy bite. Pastry crumbs fell to the table.

Heath mimicked him.

Listening as the men bantered, Reese savored her pastry between sips of coffee.

Heath's face grew serious, his joking pushed aside. "Don't leave it, Doc. Life is precious, and time is short. You never know when the woman you love will suddenly disappear from your life."

Reese shifted uncomfortably as Heath's gaze bore into hers.

Heath couldn't believe he'd pointedly stared at Reese and made such a bold statement. Did she know he was speaking of her and her sudden departure from Chapel Cove? And his life? No explanation. Just gone. Off to chase her stupid dreams.

Not that they were really stupid, and he was incredibly proud of what she'd achieved.

But if she'd only stuck around, in time she would have come to see what a beautiful life he could've given her. Sure, in hindsight it did take a number of years to establish himself, find his feet and his path, but they would've gotten there. Together.

He finished his pastry then swigged the last mouthful of coffee. "We should see if there's any update on Ivy." He eased out of his chair.

Dr. Johnson stood too and grabbed his unfinished drink. "We'll need to ask at the surgical waiting room."

Reese pushed her cup away and rose, standing tall in those high-heeled black boots, her shapely slender legs curving all the way up to the cream sweater she wore. "I'm not letting you men hear news about Aunt Ivy before me." She grabbed her jacket and bag from the back of the chair. A tan, woolen tailored coat that earlier had hung to her thighs, it was the perfect finish to her outfit. But then, she *was* a supermodel—perfection was the name of her game.

When they got to the surgical waiting room, Heath strode ahead of Dr. Johnson and Reese to the desk.

The nurse behind the desk glanced up.

Heath smiled at her. "Hi there, I was wondering if you'd be able to give me an update on a patient? Ivy Macnamara."

With a nod, she typed on her keyboard. "I'm sorry, sir, it seems she's still in surgery."

Of course, Dr. Johnson had said an hour or two, best case scenario, so it was a little early to tell. He quirked his lips and nodded. As he turned away, the receptionists' voice made him pause.

"You can wait in the family lounge. Once she's in recovery, a doctor will come and update you."

"Thank you. We'll do that." Heath turned back to Reese and Dr. Johnson.

Although the lounge was comfortable, Heath paced the floor. As did Dr. Johnson. Reese remained seated, although he didn't blame her with those heels. Then again, when she'd put them on this morning, she'd probably only intended to go to church and home again, not take a trip into the city.

Seeing a doctor in green scrubs heading their way, Heath rushed forward.

The man held out his hand and Heath shook it.

"I'm Dr. Moreno. Are you family of Ivy Macnamara?"

"Friends." Before Heath could say more, Dr. Johnson was at his side. Then Reese.

"Do you have news on Ivy?" Dr. Johnson asked.

"She's out of surgery and in recovery at the moment," the surgeon said.

"And h–her heart?" Dr. Johnson choked.

"We've managed to clear the blockage and insert a stent. She'll be transferred to the Cardiac Care Unit on the second floor shortly. There's a waiting area close to the CCU."

"Thank you, doctor." Heath glanced at Dr. Johnson, then at Reese. "We should wait there."

From where Heath sat in the small waiting area, he could see anyone coming or going from the CCU. Time ticked by slowly with little said between the trio.

Heath's ears pricked at the sound of someone approaching. When an orderly wheeled a bed around the corner toward them, Heath shot to his feet and hurried forward. An IV bag was swinging from a pole above the patient's head, and a nurse walked briskly beside them, speaking to the patient as they moved.

Standing beside him, Dr. Johnson asked anxiously, "Is that her?"

Heath shook his head. "I can't tell." He watched closely as the bed rolled by. Ivy's tired eyes caught his for a split second as they passed, and his heart squeezed. Then she was gone, swallowed by the closing doors to the CCU.

"It was her," Heath said. "She looked weary."

"She'd be groggy from the sedation," Dr. Johnson said. "Thankfully it's not a procedure requiring general anesthetic."

"Do you think they'll let us see her?" Soft floral notes wafted over Heath's shoulder.

He turned to see Reese standing right behind him. Had she just applied fresh perfume? And lipstick?

"Hmm, some hospitals have strict family protocol in the CCU."

Dr. Johnson's voice drew Heath's gaze from Reese.

"No harm in asking though," the doctor continued. "Let's just give them some time to settle her before we do so, all right?"

"Good idea." Heath closed his eyes for a moment. *Please, Reese, step away...you're driving me crazy being this close.*

As if in answer to his plea, Reese whirled around and headed back to the chair and magazine she'd been glued to since they'd arrived in the waiting area. Was that her way of coping with Ivy's situation, or had she been trying to avoid him?

"I–I'm going to grab some coffee from the coffee shop. You want one, Doc?" Heath asked.

Dr. Johnson chuckled. "There's a perfectly good machine right here, Heath."

Heath pulled a face. "I'd rather pay for a coffee than drink a cup of that brew, even if it is free."

"Well then, thank you. That would be nice." The doctor strolled back to the couches and sank into one.

Heath followed him, pausing beside Reese's chair. He cleared his throat. "Reese..."

She closed her eyes for a moment then slowly raised them to him.

Heath shifted on his feet. Why were things so awkward between them? Not that they hadn't been that way since he'd first seen her yesterday—except for the very brief moment in his truck when she'd made him laugh at the thought of being a superhero. Maybe it was because of all the years that had separated them, or the fact that she was married, or their very last encounter so long ago.

Or all of the above.

"Um, would you like another coffee?" he asked.

She shook her head. "If I have too much caffeine, I won't sleep tonight."

Best he fill up on the black brew as much as was possible then. He still had to drive everyone home safely later. And in the dark, those winding roads over the mountains and through the forests could be rather treacherous.

Dr. Johnson pressed his hands to his knees.

Heath stopped him. "Don't get up. It's only two cups—I can manage."

Desperate to clear his head, Heath took his time on the way to the coffee shop, stopping at the bathroom first. After flushing, he washed his hands then splashed his face with cold water. If only that could wake him up to the reality that Reese was a married woman. Had been for years.

Why then was she still not wearing a wedding ring? Considering who her husband was, she should've had diamonds dripping from her fingers. Yet, her fingers were bare.

All ten of them.

He couldn't shake the feeling that there was a lot more to her unjeweled state and being back in Chapel Cove than just a casual family visit and forgetting to put her rings back on. If he could scrape together enough courage, he'd ask her when they were alone.

In the coffee shop, he ordered two coffees with cream to go and then scrutinized the packaged sandwiches. Everyone must be hungry by now. That Danish pastry could only last so long.

He selected an assortment, that way he'd hopefully get someone's preference right. Reese would probably want something on the healthier side, so he chose a turkey, Swiss cheese and mustard on rye for her. For the doc, he picked a BLT baguette. Finally, for himself, a club sandwich with turkey, ham, bacon, Colby-Jack cheese, lettuce, tomato, and mayo. Hopefully nobody else would choose that one because he couldn't wait to sink his teeth into all that succulence.

As long as he didn't end up with the rye sandwich, he'd be happy. He detested rye bread.

After adding three cans of pop to the order—two of them diet options—Heath settled the bill.

Clutching the cardboard two-cup carrier tray to his chest, the disposable coffee cups securely tucked inside, he wrapped the fingers of his other hand around the brown paper bag containing their sandwiches and pop. Then he made his way back upstairs to where he'd left Reese and the doctor.

Slowly easing himself off the sofa, Dr. Johnson chuckled. "What have you got there, son? I thought you were just getting two coffees."

Heath shrugged. "I thought you and Reese might be hungry."

"Hungry?" Reese shot to her feet. "I'm famished. Thank you."

She lifted her handbag and dug inside a few moments before her cheeks flushed. She glanced up and her eyes locked with Heath's.

"I–I'll pay you back when we get home." She set the bag back down on the floor beside her chair then tucked her hair behind her ears. "I didn't bring my wallet with me. Didn't know we'd be taking a road trip today. Not that Chapel Cove to Portland is exactly a road trip."

Heath smiled. "That's all right. My treat. For both of you." Wasn't like he couldn't afford it.

Reese rubbed her hands together and bounced lightly on her heels. "So, what do you have?"

Heath set the bag and coffees down on the low table between

the seating. He handed a coffee to the doctor then rattled off the meal options.

Reese's eyes widened. She smacked her lips together. "I'll have— No, wait, did you buy anything specific for anyone?"

Heath shook his head. Well, he hadn't really, although he did have each of them in mind with his choices.

"Great! Then I'll have—" Reese groaned. "I almost forgot that my mom drummed it into me as a child—elders first. So you choose first, Dr. Johnson."

The doctor smiled. "Thank goodness your mother taught you manners, young lady. I was worried I'd be left with the turkey on rye." Wrinkling his nose, he chuckled and shook his head. "I really don't like that bread."

Neither did Heath. That flat feel on the back of your tongue...blah. And rye was also way too chewy. He was hungry. He wanted to devour his meal, not churn every piece around in his mouth a hundred times.

But, odds were now fifty-to-fifty that he might have to stomach it.

"I'll have the BLT baguette, if that's okay," Dr. Johnson said then sipped his coffee.

Heath reached into the paper bag and pulled out the baguette. He handed it to the doctor. "Of course. Enjoy it." At least he'd gotten one option right.

He turned his attention back to Reese. "And for you?" *Please, please, please say the rye.*

Reese grinned. "Can I take a peek?"

"Of course. No secrets in there." Heath unpacked the remaining two sandwiches onto the table and the three cans.

Dr. Johnson leaned forward and snagged a diet pop.

Flipping the lids of the packaging open, Reese examined the remaining two options. Almost immediately she said, "The club sandwich." She giggled. "It's bigger. I do love a good club sandwich and that one looks really good."

She lifted the foam takeout container, and before Heath could even attempt to protest, she'd taken a huge bite out of his beloved sandwich, chomping merrily on it. Not that he would've protested. He'd always had no resistance when it came to Reese.

Heath swallowed hard, the saliva sticking in his throat at the thought of eating rye. Maybe he should excuse himself and disappear back to the coffee shop to swap the sandwich. Or buy another.

Or he could be a man, suck it up, and eat the dark bread. Maybe after consuming a full rye sandwich, he'd come to enjoy its unusual flavor.

"Told you I was hungry." Reese licked some mayonnaise from the corner of her lip. "Oh, I hope you eat rye. Not everyone likes it. I do, but this sandwich trumped the two, although I *will* have to opt for the remaining diet pop."

"Help yourself," Heath replied, avoiding answering her question about the rye bread. At least he didn't get the diet pop. Yuck.

Chapter Six

REESE WIPED her hands on one of the disposable napkins she'd found inside the paper bag. "That was soooo good."

Guilt pricked her conscience. She really should have offered Heath a bite, just in case he'd been dying to taste that club sandwich. But she'd enjoyed it so much, before she realized, she'd eaten the entire thing.

"Mine was also really great, although way too big," Dr. Johnson said as he slowly rose. He shoved the remaining half of his baguette into his jacket's right pocket, the can of pop into the left one. He smiled. "Dinner. Now, I'm going to see if I can catch a nurse's attention and ask if we'd be permitted to see Ivy."

Heath and Reese pushed to their feet as well and followed the doctor to the closed frosted glass CCU doors. As Dr. Johnson reached for the buzzer, the door swung open and a stocky nurse filled the doorway.

"Can I help you?" she snapped.

Ouch. Unpleasant.

Reese narrowed her eyes. *Dragon nurse.* She clamped her teeth on her tongue to stop herself from telling the woman that a little courtesy wouldn't hurt. The title she gave the nurse did seem fitting though, and a smile twitched one corner of Reese's mouth.

"Y–yes. I'm Dr. Johnson. I was wondering if we would be able to visit with a friend of ours—Ivy Macnamara. She was brought in from surgery about forty-five minutes ago."

The nurse stared at Dr. Johnson, her gaze giving him a thorough once-over. "Are you family? Because I'm sorry but only family are permitted to visit. And only two at a time."

"I'm her niece." The words shot out of Reese's mouth before she'd even thought them through. Well, she could be. Aunt Ivy was like family to her. She just hoped pretending to be her niece didn't jeopardize Nai's chances of getting in. But then, Aunt Ivy certainly could have more than one niece. As long as Aunt Ivy doesn't tell the staff she only has one.

Just in case, Reese muttered, "My, um…cousin, Nai, will be here tomorrow."

"All right, you can come in," the nurse said to Reese. "You'll need to sanitize your hands first."

As Reese nodded, her nose suddenly tickled then burned. She covered her mouth as she sneezed. Oh no, was she coming down with a cold? Must be from her run yesterday, or getting slightly wet in the rain as she bolted from Heath's truck into her parents' house.

Or she was just allergic to hospitals. Or this nurse.

Dragon nurse glared at Reese. "Are you ill?"

Reese shook her head slowly from side to side. "No…"

"Well, we can't take a chance. Best you put on gloves and a

mask as well. Wait here and I'll get some for you." She disappeared into the CCU, reappearing moments later. She handed the protective clothing to Reese then shifted her attention to Heath and Dr. Johnson. "And you? Are you family? If you are, only one of you will be able to go in with her niece."

Heath shook his head. "Just a friend."

Stupid. Why didn't Heath say he was her pastor? Surely he'd gain access that way? Then again, he *was* a youth pastor, wasn't he? And Aunt Ivy didn't exactly fall into the youth category. Likely Heath would never lie now that he was a man of the cloth. Come to think of it, all the years she'd known him, he'd always been rather upright and honest. Except for the fact that he'd watched that R-rated movie when he wasn't old enough.

"I–I'm her fiancé," Dr. Johnson said. "As well as her GP."

Reese and Heath's gazes collided for a second before they both focused on the doctor, jaws dropping.

Dr. Johnson merely tipped his chin as if challenging them to correct his untruth. Well, at least one part of his answer was a lie.

With a harrumph, dragon nurse eyed him. "So long as you don't attempt to tell us how to do our jobs in there, Dr. Johnson, as soon as Mrs. Macnamara's niece is masked and gloved, you can enter. The patient's room is the second door on the right." Then she walked away from them and the CCU. If she didn't return, Heath could maybe slip in after she'd seen Aunt Ivy. *If* his conscience would allow him.

"Fiancé?" Heath chuckled. "That's certainly moving things fast from planning to declare your feelings."

"Well, Ivy likely would've been if I hadn't dragged my feet for years," Dr. Johnson muttered.

Reese let out a soft groan. Two of her fingers had ended up in the same sheath. She tugged on the empty slot where her finger should have been, trying her best not to puncture the nitrile glove.

It was so difficult to get these things on with her long nails.

"Here, let me help you with that." Heath took her hand.

In no time, blue nitrile covered the skin of all five fingers. He did the same with her other hand, and Reese found herself strangely disappointed when he released her fingers.

"You coming, slow poke?" Dr. Johnson's eyes twinkled with his smile. Reese would be surprised if there wasn't a proposal before the week ended.

Fastening the mask over her nose and mouth, Reese scooted closer. "Well, you're just the eager beaver, that's all. Can't help it you can't wait to see your *fiancée*," she teased as she followed him inside the CCU.

Just as dragon nurse had said, Aunt Ivy's dimly lit room wasn't far from the entrance. When Reese neared the bed, she gasped. Aunt Ivy looked so frail in the bed, hooked up to an IV and monitors. "W–what's making those noises?" she whispered to Dr. Johnson.

"Just the heart and BP monitors."

He allowed Reese to step up to the bed while he remained behind her in the shadows. Was he just being polite, or was he afraid to look too closely at the woman he loved. He would be able to read far more into Aunt Ivy's condition than she could.

Reese took Aunt Ivy's limp hand in hers.

For a brief moment, Aunt Ivy's eyes flickered open then closed again. A soft smile brushed her lips. "Nai…?"

"No, Aunt Ivy, i–it's Reese."

The older woman's brows drew together momentarily as she frowned. Then she squeezed Reese's hand. "Clarise…sweet girl…it's g–good to see you…" Her words slurred. She *was* groggy, and Reese wondered how much longer she'd remain so sleepy.

Aunt Ivy opened her mouth again and mumbled, "W–what

happened?"

Dr. Johnson hurried to the other side of the bed, opposite Reese. Positioning himself close to Aunt Ivy's head, he gently combed his fingers through her gray hair. "You suffered a heart attack, Ivy. But you're going to be fine. The surgeons have cleared the blockage and inserted a stent."

Aunt Ivy shifted her sleepy gaze to where Dr. Johnson stood. "Jeff? I–is that...you?"

"It's me, Ivy." Dr. Johnson brushed his hand over her head once more.

"W–what are you...doing here?" Aunty Ivy struggled with her speech.

Reese looked on in wonder as he sweetly smiled at her, love radiating from his eyes. How had Aunt Ivy not yet guessed that this man was crazy about her?

What she wouldn't give to be loved like that.

"I'm your doctor, and your friend. I wouldn't be anywhere else at this moment." Bending closer, he lowered his voice. Reese could only just make out him saying, "Although as far as the nurses are concerned, I'm your fiancé. It was the only way I could get in to see you."

Aunt Ivy offered Dr. Johnson a sleepy smile. "Oh you..."

"Just rest now, Ivy. I'm going to be here until you tell me to go." He squeezed her shoulder.

Speaking of going, she should leave the two of them alone. She had no right to be in here, but she was glad that she had at least been able to see her friend's aunt. Now she could let Nai know how Aunt Ivy was doing.

Reese leaned forward and kissed the older woman's brow, the mask preventing her lips from touching Aunty Ivy's skin. "I should go and leave you to rest. Nai will be here as soon as she can get a flight. And just in case anyone asks, I'm your niece too."

Aunt Ivy managed a weak chuckle. "Fibbers... But I'm glad you did, although you will need to ask God's forgiveness." She closed her eyes, and soon a soft snore accompanied her breathing.

"I–I'm going to give you and Aunt Ivy time alone." Reese turned to go then paused, a grin widening across her face. "And Dr. Johnson, we don't want to see you again until you've told her how you feel."

Don't make the same mistakes I have.

She swallowed hard. Then with a quick cluck-cluck aimed at Dr. Johnson, a feeble attempt to lighten her mood, Reese strode away toward the exit.

Toward Heath.

Her heart beat faster despite her willing it not to. Why, oh why, had she ever left Chapel Cove? If she'd stayed, she and Heath would've been married and had a couple of kids who would've been teenagers by now. He'd said he wanted to marry her, and not just because of what had happened between them that night. He'd said he loved her...always had, always would.

Did he still?

She blinked back the tears burning her eyes. Everything she'd ever really hankered after since leaving Chapel Cove had been right here in front of her all along in Heath. If not for her stupid ambition, they could've lived happily ever after.

Hearing the CCU door open, Heath cut short his prayer. He glanced up to see Reese ripping off her mask and gloves and throwing them into the trash can. She dabbed the corners of her eyes, and his heart lurched. Was she crying? Just how bad was Ivy?

Heath shot to his feet as Reese looked up.

Spotting him, she froze. Her eyes darted up and down the corridor, and then she glanced over her shoulder. If he didn't know better, he'd think she was looking for a quick escape.

He hurried closer. "Reese? Are you all right? Is it Ivy?"

Without answering, she lowered her head, shaking it from side to side.

What was that? *She* wasn't okay, or Ivy was worse than anticipated?

Whatever the answer, something had clearly upset her.

Instinctively, he wrapped his arms around Reese and pulled her close, savoring the warmth of her nearness. As he smoothed a hand down her long strawberry-blond hair, as silky as he remembered, Heath resisted the urge to plant a kiss on her head.

Standing almost as tall as he, she melted into his shoulder. "I–I'm so sorry."

Icy claws dug into his stomach. "Ivy…is she…?"

"Resting. She's still a little groggy from the sedation."

Heath breathed a sigh of relief. "But I'm confused, what are you sorry about?"

Teary eyes lifted to meet his gaze. "For hurting you. For walking out on you so long ago without a word, without explaining, without giving you a chance to convince me to stay."

She regretted the choices she'd made?

Or did she merely need to get the guilt off her chest once and for all for just disappearing on him? He'd heard from Kristina and Nai that some agent in New York had contacted her after she'd sent in her portfolio. He'd considered following Reese to the Big Apple, but knew he could never compete with her dreams.

He shouldn't have taken those portfolio photos of her, even though that had been the moment when he'd realized he, too, had talent.

"It's okay. Water under the bridge. And hey, both our lives

turned out okay. I might never have become a youth pastor. And you…you would never have become a supermodel if you had stayed in that sleepy little hollow of a town." She'd been made for far greater things than Chapel Cove, it seemed.

Reese nodded and squirmed out of his embrace.

It hurt to let her go. He would've liked to have kept her there forever.

"Do you want to sit?" He gestured toward the waiting area.

She shook her head. "I–I need to get out of here."

She took off down the corridor, her heels clicking against the hard, glossy tiles.

"Wait!" Heath rushed back to grab their jackets and Reese's bag that lay on the floor beside the chair Reese had been sitting in. The one he'd occupied when she'd gone in to see Ivy.

He ran to catch up to her. Boy, for someone in heels, she certainly moved fast.

Reese slowed her pace when they came to the stairwell, taking each descending step carefully.

Much as he would've liked to help her navigate the stairs, Heath kept his hands to himself. It hurt too much to be so near her and not be able to express how much he still loved her. So much for burying his feelings all those years ago. Seemed it hadn't helped one bit.

If only she wasn't still married.

Back on the first floor, they walked in silence until they were outside. The sound of sirens wailing to a stop around the back of the hospital where the ER was situated shattered the quietude. Heath shot a prayer to heaven for the patient inside that ambulance and their family.

Rain had fallen during the hours they'd spent inside the hospital, and the parking lot asphalt glistened. Heath paused, glancing left, then right. He looked at Reese. "Where do you want to go?"

Reese shrugged. "Anywhere but inside. The walls were starting to close in on me."

"There's a park about a block away—I saw it as we drove in. We could stroll through there if you like."

She nodded.

The cool early April air nipped at Heath's skin as they walked across the parking lot. Only then did it strike him that their jackets were still safely tucked beneath his arm.

He paused and shoved his jacket between his knees. He opened Reese's coat. "Here, put this on. You're going to need it."

Reese turned and shrugged into the woolen garment, flicking her hair over her collar.

Heath smoothed his hands down her arms. "Better?"

She glanced over her shoulder and offered him a weak smile. "Much better. Thank you."

"You're welcome." Now that she was warm, he could put on his own jacket.

Heath waited until they were in the peace and tranquility of the park before asking, "Tell me more about your visit with Ivy."

Reese pointed to a nearby bench. "Let's sit first. My feet are killing me."

It had been quite a walk from the second floor of the hospital, and in those boots, Heath wasn't surprised that her feet were sore. He might just have to carry her back. The thought made his pulse beat faster.

After they'd settled onto the bench, Reese turned to him. A smile curved her full mouth.

"At first I got a fright when I saw Aunt Ivy. She looked so frail and helpless lying there in the bed with machines beeping around her, lines and numbers bouncing up and down on the monitors. But she's going to be okay. I'm certain of it. She definitely hasn't lost her bluff, despite her ordeal." Reese chuckled. "Called me and Dr. Johnson fibbers, and that we needed to repent, after I told her I was her niece and the doctor told her he was her fiancé."

Heath's eyes widened. "What? He didn't waste any time, did he?"

Reese shook her head. "Oh no, he wasn't declaring his love for her. Merely letting her know it was the only way he could get in to see her."

She rubbed her hands together then blew on them.

"You cold?"

Reese nodded. "I should've brought my gloves, hat and scarf, but I left them in my parents' car."

At least Reese had remembered what was *really* important...perfume and lipstick.

Heath tried not to smile. Much as he would've loved to have teased her about her priorities, he didn't. Instead he cupped her hands in his. "Warmer?"

She flashed him a glance. "Given time, I'm sure they will be."

Heath swallowed the lump that had formed in his throat. He shouldn't have taken her hands, but she'd seemed cold. He was just being his usual thoughtful self. And now his heart was paying the price as it pounded wildly in his chest.

Slowly Reese's gaze returned to fix on him. "Do you think he'll declare his love for her?"

"Dr. Johnson? I certainly hope so, but I'm not holding my breath that the reticence of all these years will magically vanish overnight. As Ivy strengthens, his resolve may just weaken."

Like his? Would he find the courage to ask Reese about her life?

He had to. He had to know if she was still married, divorced, or widowed.

Today.

CHAPTER SEVEN

"I–IT'S GETTING pretty cold out here. Do you mind if we go back?" Despite the fact that she'd started to shiver, Reese eased away from Heath's warm clasp. She rose and shoved her hands in her jacket pockets. Not nearly as warm as Heath's touch, but this was probably safer.

"Sure." Heath pushed to his feet.

The walk back to the parking lot was brisk—far quicker than the one to the green park where spring flowers bloomed. And once again, they strode in silence. Heath seemed to have something weighing on his mind. Well, not her problem. She had enough of her own. Like losing everything. Plus, now she needed to find a job and a place to stay. Soon. Not to mention needing to get a set of wheels of some sort to get around, possibly furnish a home... And all on her dwindling five thousand dollars. She had absolutely no idea how she was going to pull off any of that. She didn't have the drive or the courage she'd had when she was eighteen.

Inside the hospital, Heath paused and turned to Reese. "Coffee? Hot chocolate?"

"That would be wonderful. And I promise I will pay you back."

"You don't have to. Really. It's just coffee. And I am glad to have the company while I wait for Dr. Johnson."

He was? Didn't seem like it. But then, they hadn't really had time to talk privately yet, with the doctor there, then her going in to see Aunty Ivy, and then wanting to go for a walk outside where it was way too cold to be anyway. And of course, he must be worried about Aunt Ivy. Seemed they'd gotten close because of his uncle. Maybe talking was what she and Heath needed to break the strained atmosphere between them.

The coffee shop was surprisingly full. What had happened in the short time they'd been gone? Heath indicated an open booth near the back. "Should we sit there?"

"Looks great."

By the time they got to the booth, Reese had eased out of her coat. She shimmied onto the faux leather bench, placing her coat beside her.

Heath took off his jacket too, then set it down on the seat opposite her. "So, have you decided yet what you're drinking?"

Reese gazed up at him. He really was tall. And he'd aged well, like a good wine. She placed a finger over her lips and feigned thought. "Um, I think I'll have a hot chocolate to warm me up. Thank you."

Heath nodded and walked over to the counter. Soon he returned with two identical drinks. He set them down on the table, shifted his jacket over on the bench, then sat down. "I decided the hot chocolate sounded too good to resist."

Reese lifted the extra-large disposable cup to her nose. "Smells divine." She took a sip of the hot drink and smiled. "Mmm, delicious."

Heath began to chuckle as she set her cup down. "You've got some foam on your top lip."

"Oh." She laughed and licked her lip.

When Heath's chortles eased to a stop, his expression grew serious. Eyes fixed on Reese, he leaned forward. "Can I ask you something...personal?"

Large amber eyes stared back at Heath. Would she say no? Hightail it out of the hospital again? Wouldn't be the first time she'd run out on him.

He reached for her hand. "Reese?"

She pulled away and tucked her hair behind her ears. "Um, yes, of course. As long as it's not *too* personal."

Heath eased back into his seat. "Well, I hope not."

Reese took another sip of her drink. "This is really good."

Was she trying to change the subject, keeping the walls around her up?

He swallowed hard. Couldn't chicken out now. There were things he had to know—like what she was doing back in Chapel Cove? How long she planned to stay. Was she still married? Divorced? Widowed? Did she have any children?

If there was any chance that Reese was free, he wouldn't want to miss the opportunity to be a part of her life again just because he hadn't spoken up soon enough.

"I couldn't help noticing that you're not wearing a wedding ring," he began.

Instinctively, Reese covered her bare left fingers with her right hand, her gaze lowering.

"Are you—?"

"Divorced," she blurted out. "February."

Ouch, still so fresh.

His heart ached at her news. No wonder she often got that sad look on her face. Even though hurting for her pain, a sense of hope filled Heath at the same time. Maybe he could try to win her heart again. But would she be open to another relationship so soon, especially with the man she'd run from so long ago? Clearly, despite her declarations of love back then, she hadn't loved him enough to stay.

"I'm so sorry to hear that," he said.

Liar.

Reese tipped her head. "It happens. And it was inevitable."

"How long were you married for?" As if he didn't know. The grand affair when Reese tied the knot was splashed across umpteen magazines.

A bitter smile flashed across her lips. "Almost fifteen years."

"Was he…" Heath touched her hand lightly, "abusive to you?"

Reese's eyes widened, but she didn't pull away this time. "Abusive? Humph, no! Lloyd would *never* do anything to damage his investment."

While her husband may not have scarred her physically, she certainly seemed to carry some kind of emotional scars.

"So, why did your marriage end?" Heath had seen images of them on social media and in magazines, and they had always looked so happy—dubbed 'The Golden Couple of the Fashion World'.

Her shoulders lifted in a shrug. "The age-old problem…traded me in for a younger model. Pfft, or rather, way too many test drives over far too many years."

What man in his right mind would cheat on someone as beautiful and full of life as Reese Aylward? What he wouldn't do to reach across the table, draw her into his arms, and kiss all the hurt away. At the same time, part of him wished he could ask her if it had been worth it—the fame, the bright lights, leaving him—and whether she would go back to New York once she had healed.

Did he even dare put his heart on the line again for this woman? *Yes! A million times yes!*

But instead of vocalizing his thoughts, Heath said, "I'm sorry to hear that."

His thumb smoothed across the top of her hand. "Were you ever happy with him?"

She cocked her head. "Hmm, a year or two, maybe. Then I just kept hoping things would change. Finally, I ran out of hope."

"Did you have any children together?"

Reese swallowed and looked away. Slowly, her hand slid from beneath his.

Had he said the wrong thing? Hit a nerve?

"Reese?"

She glanced back at him and blinked away the moisture in her eyes. "I–I thought you wanted to ask me some*thing*. That's been a whole lot of things," she snapped.

She shouldn't have been so short with Heath. He meant well. But how could she not when he'd touched on her most sensitive heartache?

Children...

Sadness overwhelmed Reese once again. How *could* she have children when her husband kept moving the goalposts? Kept breaking his promises? She'd heard Lloyd's empty words for over ten years, and they still caused bile to rise in her throat.

"When you turn thirty, honey...your career is still booming.

Why risk all you've worked so hard for? There's still plenty of time for motherhood."

And when thirty came, it was thirty-three. Then thirty-five. Thirty-eight. Now she was staring down the barrel of her fortieth birthday, childless.

She swallowed back her tears.

"Reese?"

Heath's gentle, warm touch on her hand sent tingles through her body once again.

"No children. There, are you satisfied? And if I did have, none of them would've been yours." Was that the question he'd really wanted to ask? Did you leave Chapel Cove because you were pregnant? Well she hadn't been. Opportunity had knocked way sooner than she thought it would, and she'd had dreams to follow. She couldn't risk everything she'd ever wanted for Heath Brock.

"I–I'm sorry. The last thing I wanted to do was hurt or offend you." Heath's gaze lowered until he was staring at the table, the look on his face one of genuine regret.

Reese shook her head. "No, I'm sorry. I should never have snapped at you—twice. It was a legitimate question. After all these years, it's natural to want to know these things."

She stretched out her legs, and as she did, her calf brushed against Heath's.

A smile twitched at the corners of his mouth.

Shifting her legs fractionally away, she asked, "So, what about you?"

He glanced up at her. "What about me?"

"Are you married?"

Heath shook his head. "No."

"Divorced too? Because I totally get that. So many people our age have tried marriage, just to find it didn't work out. There's Kristina who's also recently divorced. Maybe Nai had the right idea in never getting married."

"I've never been married," Heath answered. "And I don't have any children either, in case that question was coming next."

A strange feeling of relief filled Reese that Heath was still single. She stared at him. "Seriously? Never married?" Then again, if he had been married, surely he would've upgraded from his bachelor pad on the beach.

Eyes fixed on hers, his gaze bore into her very soul. "How could I marry? I've only ever loved one woman."

CHAPTER EIGHT

HEATH'S WORDS had swirled in Reese's mind as they'd whiled away an hour or two in the coffee shop. He'd told her he loved her long, long ago. Was he referring to her when he said he'd only ever loved one woman? And did that mean he *still* loved her?

Finally, they wandered upstairs to the CCU again. Every chair in the small waiting area was full.

The people sitting there seemed to know each other. Could they be family and friends of the patient who was in the ambulance when she and Heath had stepped out earlier? Well, whoever they were, they were well and truly settled in those seats.

She turned to Heath. "Looks as if we're going to have to find another place to sit and wait."

"Sure does. We could go back to the coffee shop."

"What about your truck?" Reese hurriedly asked, tired of being inside the hospital. "At least it'll be quiet if we want to get some sleep. I'm feeling pretty exhausted."

"We could do that…if you don't mind being in a confined space with me."

Why would she mind? Although, the last time they were in a confined space together, she'd lost her virginity. Not entirely Heath's fault though. She had wanted him as much as he'd wanted her. But that was a lifetime ago. They'd grown up. They'd changed. Plus, Heath had found God too. Ironic that she was now the one disconnected from the Almighty. Was it possible for her to find her way back to Him again in Chapel Cove? Could Heath be the one to show her the way? Now that would be a reversal of roles. As teens, she'd been the one to encourage him to give his life to God.

"Of course I don't mind," Reese replied. "We've pretty much spent the day together and survived."

His lips curved in a smile and her heart did another of those somersaults it had started doing today.

"I promise to behave," Heath said. "And I do have a thick blanket behind the seat if you get cold, although I can also run the heater if it gets *too* chilly. Bonus is that we'd have the radio to listen to—I always find music soothing to the soul."

Reese returned his smile. "Sounds good. Why don't you quickly pop in and see Ivy? While you're there, you can let Dr. Johnson know where we'll be waiting."

"I–I couldn't. Much as I'd love to. I'm not family." Heath touched her shoulder. "You go in and let him know."

"Hey, I'm not family either. You're probably closer to family than I am. If Aunt Ivy had hooked up with your uncle and married him, you would've been her nephew. Not your fault life took that away from you. And besides, you *are* a pastor at the church she attends."

"A *youth* pastor," Heath argued.

Reese closed her eyes for a moment, tipped her chin, and shrugged. "What does that matter? You're a pastor, and I'm sure Ivy would appreciate not only seeing you, but also having you pray for her. I'll wait here and offer up a few prayers that dragon nurse isn't anywhere around."

Brow raised, Heath chuckled. "Dragon nurse?"

"My nickname for the battle-ax we had to get past to get into the CCU earlier."

"I'll be sure not to call her that if I bump into her." Heath sanitized his hands and pressed the buzzer to the CCU.

A young nurse opened the door, smiled, and without asking any questions, let Heath inside.

Reese was certain that Heath had shot a prayer to heaven himself asking for easy access.

Following Reese's directions to Ivy's room, Heath tiptoed inside, toward her bed.

That was easy. *Thank you, Lord. You are forever faithful.*

"How is she?" he whispered to Dr. Johnson, seated in a chair beside Ivy, holding her hand.

The doctor looked up. "Heath... I'm so glad you managed to get in."

"I won't stay long. I just wanted to quickly pray with Ivy." Heath stepped up close to the bed and brushed his hand lightly over Ivy's gray head.

Dr. Johnson nodded. "I know she'll appreciate that. Thank you."

"So, how is she?" Heath asked again.

"She's doing really well, considering we almost lost her. She's been asleep most of the time I've been here. Must've been quite a strong sedative they gave her. Still waiting for her cardiologist to check in on her."

Heath pursed his lips. "So I guess you haven't been able to tell her yet how you feel?"

Mouth downturned, the doctor shook his head. "Unfortunately not." His eyes lit with a smile. "One good thing, her heart monitor responds positively when I talk to her. I'm optimistic that I'll get a chance to tell her before we return to Chapel Cove."

"Just don't get cold feet when the opportunity arises, Doc."

"I won't. I've wasted too much time already." Dr. Johnson brushed his hand gently up and down Ivy's arm. "So, what time do you want to leave?"

"We'll stay as long as you need to. It's my day off tomorrow and Reese isn't working, so we're not in any hurry to get back."

A soft chuckle spilled from the elderly man's mouth. "I bet you aren't."

Cocking his head to the side, Heath frowned. What did he mean by that?

"If you don't mind me saying, I couldn't help noticing that there's strong chemistry between you and Reese. Do you have feelings for her?"

When it came to matters of the heart, the doc was sharp for someone his age.

Heath nodded. "She's the only girl I've ever loved."

"And, do you still love her?"

He couldn't deny it. He'd never stopped loving Reese.

"Yes, I do."

The graying head moved up and down slowly. "Then take some advice from your doctor and take a big old spoonful of your own medicine, okay? Cold feet can only lead to a whole lot of other ailments, like a pining or broken heart."

Heath's mouth curved at the good advice. "Touché, Doc. I'll be sure to follow your orders."

Resting a hand on Ivy's shoulder, Heath said, "Shall we pray?"

"Please do." Dr. Johnson bowed his head and closed his eyes.

Heath did the same and began to pray. "Dear Lord Jesus, thank You for saving Ivy's life today. Yes, we all did our part with the skills that You have graciously given us—Dr. Johnson, Riley, Pete, the medevac staff, the surgeons, myself…even Reese—but ultimately, Lord, we could not have done it without Your sustaining strength.

"Please bring complete healing to Ivy, and Lord—" Dare he even make this request? Why not? God was interested in every part of each person's existence, no matter how small. "Please work out these complicated love lives of Dr. Johnson and myself.

"But, Lord, in all things, as always, not our will but Yours be done.

"I pray this in the name of the Father, and of the Son, and of the Holy Spirit. Amen."

"Amen," Dr. Johnson repeated. "Thank you, Heath."

"It was my honor. And now, I'm going to leave you with Ivy. Please, stay as long as you like. Reese and I will be in the truck since the waiting area outside is full. Seems there was some kind of an emergency earlier. I'm sure there'll be another patient along here soon enough." Heath turned to go.

Dr. Johnson stopped him as he gripped Heath's arm. "Won't you be cold out there in the truck? Or is that the idea? Have her snuggle up to you for warmth, eh Romeo?" He waggled his brows.

Hmm, not a bad idea at all. And now Heath was even more convinced that the old guy hadn't lost his sense of romance.

Hopefully, Heath hadn't either, and he could win Reese's love again.

He smiled at the doctor. "We'll be fine. I have heat in the truck *and* a blanket." At the image of sharing the warmth with Reese, Heath couldn't help but return the doctor's brow waggle.

As they passed the coffee shop on their way out, Heath asked Reese if she was hungry. Who knew when the coffee shop would close? Although they could always drive and find a Starbucks.

She offered him a sheepish smile. "A little. It must be almost time for dinner. Maybe I should go back to CCU and ask Dr. Johnson to join us."

"I'm sure he'll come down and grab a bite when he's ready. And he does still have his pop and leftover baguette. It is, of course, entirely possible that he may not wish to leave Ivy's side for a moment until he has to. I know if it were me in his position, I wouldn't want to." Heath grinned. "We could be in for a long night."

"No problem. I'll just call my parents when we have a better idea of when we're returning home."

Back inside the coffee shop, they scanned the menus. It didn't take long for Heath to shut his and slide it across the table away from him.

Reese glanced up at him. "You already know what you want?"

"Yup. One of those club sandwiches you had for lunch."

Reese narrowed her gaze. "That was *your* sandwich I ate at lunch, wasn't it?"

Heath burst out laughing. "Well, it didn't officially have my name on it, but..." Leaning over the table, he whispered in her ear. "Can I make a confession?"

She nodded.

"I hate rye bread."

"What?" Reese gave him a playful smack on the arm. "Why

didn't you tell me? I would've traded meals."

"And rob me of the joy of watching you devour that club sandwich, mayo dripping down your chin? No way. Besides, I'll get my turn to taste it soon."

"I did *not* have mayonnaise dripping down my chin. Only a little at the corner of my mouth. Once." Reese's chuckle was like a babbling brook on a summer's day. "But it was soooo good, I don't mind eating it again. So make that two. I look forward to savoring that deliciousness."

After they'd eaten and had a pit stop at the bathroom, Heath grabbed two coffees to go, a large slab of chocolate, and some pop. They hurried back to his truck and quickly slid inside, out of the cold night air.

Twisting around, Heath rested one knee on the seat and reached behind the backrest. He pulled out the blanket he always kept there for emergencies, then spread it over Reese's legs.

She clasped the soft fabric between her fingers and lifted it higher over her body. Drawing it to her nose, she took a deep whiff.

Thankfully he'd stopped by Uncle Trafford's house on Friday to do laundry after returning from his road trip to California to see Hunter. The blanket had been given a wash too.

She turned to him and smiled. "Hmm, fresh. I'm impressed." The same mischief he'd grown to love so long ago in a twelve-year old glinted in her amber eyes.

He cracked a grin. "Hey, I might live in a camper, but I'm no slob. I love fresh bedding as much as the next person."

"Don't I know…"

Reese quickly looked away, seeming to realize what she'd said.

Heat crept up Heath's neck. He shifted uncomfortably on the seat. Could they ever get over what had happened that night?

He cleared his throat. "Reese… I am sorry about what happened between us. Truly. If I could go back in time and have that Valentine's Day over, I would do everything differently." He would have taken her home to her parents' house after their romantic dinner, not to his camper. He would've kissed her goodnight before seeing her safely in and not allowed their desires to get the better of them.

She shrugged then slowly returned his gaze. "I–I'm not sure I would've wanted it any different. Nothing would've changed my ambitions, my dreams, or the letter that arrived from New York not long after." Her eyes searched his. "At least we'll always have that one night."

Oh, he had wanted so many more nights with her. Still did. But as her husband.

He leaned closer to her, and his hand cupped her cheek. He had ached for her for so many years, it was hard to believe that she was right there beside him, in his truck.

Dare he try to kiss her?

Before he could even take action on that thought, Reese shifted closer and slid her hand around his neck, her eyes searching his uncertainly. Their mouths were now so close he could feel her warm breath against his skin.

And then their lips touched, lightly at first, their passion igniting with each passing second. He wrapped her in his embrace, and all the years melted away. Heath was twenty-one again.

What was she doing? Her heart pounding, Reese told herself that she should stop, but oh, she just couldn't. And she couldn't deny that those old feelings for Heath had never really gone away, even after more than two decades.

Had she been the one to initiate the kiss? Or Heath?

Did it matter? She was back home to sort her life out, once and for all, a task way overdue. It wouldn't help her one bit to make the same mistakes all over again.

But Heath had promised to behave himself. She believed him. She trusted him. And they *were* only kissing.

Just as you were when you were nearly eighteen...

Pulling away from him was just as difficult as it had been that long ago night. She could feast on these kisses forever.

No! Stop this now, Reese, before it gets out of hand.

Reluctantly, Reese broke the kiss and eased out of Heath's arms before temptation got the better of one of them. Trailing a finger over her bottom lip, she stared out of the windshield. Already the window had begun to mist up.

She glanced Heath's way as he leaned into the backrest and released a heavy sigh. He raked his fingers through his hair.

Turning his head, his eyes found hers, and regret clouded his green gaze. "I–I'm so sorry, Reese. I'd promised to behave, and I didn't."

She reached for his hand and gave it a light squeeze before releasing it. "You did behave. I'm the one who started this. I kissed you first."

Heath chuckled. "Well, I think we both kissed each other at the same time."

She smiled. "You're right. But it probably is a bad idea. And I do need to call Nai and give her an update on Aunt Ivy. And my parents. I probably should've done it when you went in to pray for Aunt Ivy, but I wanted to wait for your feedback first."

Reese retrieved her cell phone from her jacket pocket then dialed her friend's number, already missing being in Heath's arms and kicking herself for pulling away from him.

CHAPTER NINE

REESE WOKE to a knocking sound. She cracked her eyes open. Darkness surrounded her, and it was cold. Heath must've turned off the truck to save gas after she'd fallen asleep.

What was going on? Where was she?

She pulled the blanket higher, glancing toward the source of the noise. Beyond Heath's profile, someone rapped on the misted window.

"Heath! Reese!" came the muffled voice.

Heath? Like a chicken coming home to roost, she'd found her way back into his arms sometime during the night, their faces so close she could reach up and kiss him…again.

It all flooded back to her. After Reese had called Nai and her friend informed her she could only get an early morning flight out of Austin, Heath cranked the engine and turned on the heater.

While savoring the warmth the hot air offered, they'd finished their drinks, as well as the chocolate slab. Heath insisted they should as the heat would melt the chocolate. She didn't mind at all—she loved chocolate—although she was certain the only thing the heat had melted was her. She'd soon grown sleepy, drifting off not long after the last delectable, creamy block had tickled her taste buds.

The knock came again, louder this time.

Heath's eyes shot open and he bolted upright.

Reese's arm fell from his taut waist, regret filling her at the loss of her muscular, but oh-so-comfortable pillow. She inched away as Heath rolled down the window to Dr. Johnson's smiling face.

"Good morning," the old man said, way too cheery for Reese's liking.

"Morning, Doc," Heath replied.

"What time is it?" Reese muttered with a yawn as she put some distance between her and Heath.

"Five-forty." Dr. Johnson hurried around the truck to the passenger side. He opened the door and slid inside, forcing Reese to shimmy close to Heath again. "Sorry, it's getting chilly standing outside."

Acutely aware of the feel of Heath beside her, Reese shivered. She liked that feeling. Very much.

"Morning or evening?" she mumbled. She'd so lost track of time.

A loud laugh spewed from the doctor's mouth. "It's morning, my dear girl. I came by around eleven last night, but you were both fast asleep. So I just left you and went back to Ivy. I'm glad I did, because she woke up around three—as in wide awake. Suddenly, she wanted to chat."

Heath leaned forward, keeping his eyes fixed on Dr. Johnson. "Don't keep us in suspense. Did you tell Ivy how you feel about her? Did you declare your undying love?"

Dr. Johnson pulled a face at Heath's choice of words. "Perhaps that wouldn't have been the best phrase for me to use with Ivy…considering the circumstances."

Heath's laugh filled the cabin. "You're so right, Doc. But you know what I mean."

"I know, son." The doctor's smile quickly disappeared. He pursed his lips and shook his head. "But sadly, no. To reveal my true feelings to Ivy in a hospital after all this time just didn't seem…romantic enough. Besides, she's got her spunk back and kicked me out before I had a chance to change my mind."

Heath smiled. "Spunk, huh? I guess that means she's recovering well?"

Dr. Johnson tipped his head back and let out a long sigh. "Oh, yes… She told me I had to leave because there were patients back in Chapel Cove who needed me. The more I tried to explain that the clinic was covered and that she also needed me, the more Ivy insisted she was fine and didn't need a babysitter. Sometimes that woman is totally insufferable."

"But you love her." Heath's gaze flitted to Reese.

With a smile and a nod, Dr. Johnson replied, "But I love her."

Reese's heart warmed. *How sweet.* Would Heath have said those three magical words to her last night if she hadn't pulled away from him?

"So, I guess we're ready to head back home then?" Heath reached for the ignition.

Reese gripped his hand to stop him. "Not so fast, cowboy. I'd like to stop at the ladies room before we hit the road. That hot chocolate from last night hasn't gone straight to my hips, I promise."

Of course… She hadn't been to the bathroom since just before they returned to the car last night, while he had slipped out when she was fast asleep.

"Good idea. But let me at least park closer so we don't have that far to walk in the dark and cold." Heath started the engine then turned to Dr. Johnson. "You need to go, doc?"

"No. I went just before I came outside to wake you." Dr. Johnson leaned his head against the post. "If you don't mind, I got very little sleep last night, so I'll need to get some shuteye."

Heath nodded and started the engine.

Taking the blanket from her legs, Reese scrunched it up into a makeshift pillow. She handed it to the doctor. "Use this. It's way softer and warmer than that metal post. Besides, Heath can put on the heater if we get cold."

Reese always did have a soft side to her harder exterior. It was one of the things Heath had loved so much about her. He was glad to see she hadn't lost that trait.

"Thank you, my dear. That's very kind of you." Dr. Johnson shoved the blanket beneath his head and then sank his head into its softness. With a contented sigh, he closed his eyes.

Heath pulled the truck to a stop in front of the hospital entrance, and Reese followed him out the driver's side. Once they'd both freshened up in the bathroom, they hit the road.

After a little small talk, silence descended on the cabin. And stayed there pretty much all the way back to Chapel Cove. Except for the phone call from Nai when they were well over halfway home. Her plane had just landed in Phoenix. Reese gave her a quick update on Ivy and then she folded her arms and closed her eyes.

With the soft light of dawn breaking, Heath was thankful they'd waited until the morning to leave. The sun had risen by the time they were almost halfway back home. He didn't have to navigate those forest roads in the dark.

In the silence, thoughts of their kiss the night before consumed his mind. Reese *had* started it. *She* was the one who had embraced him first, neared his lips.

Did that mean she was still attracted to him? Bigger question, how deep did that attraction go? Could he even dare to hope that she'd buried her feelings for him all these years—that yesterday had unearthed them?

But what did she mean by saying their kissing was probably a bad idea? It wasn't as if she was married anymore, and by the sounds of it, her marriage had been over for years.

He shot Reese a glance. She'd fallen asleep about a half hour ago. But now, she rested her head on the doctor's shoulder. If only she had chosen his shoulder instead, as she had last night.

Heath decided to drop the doc off first. He wanted to speak to Reese alone before returning her to her parents' house.

He reached out and gave her a light shake. "Reese, we're back in Chapel Cove."

Stirring, she slowly righted herself then rubbed her eyes. She ruffled her fingers through her hair and muttered, "Ugh, I must look a mess."

Heath smiled at her. "You look beautiful. As always."

She dug her elbow into his ribs. "Liar."

"Never!"

She returned his grin.

Heath sucked in a breath and exhaled. "Please would you wake Dr. Johnson? I need to find out if he wants to be dropped at the clinic or his house."

The instant Reese shook Dr. Johnson's shoulder and spoke his name, his eyes shot open. He looked around, bewildered.

"Morning, Doc. Have a good sleep?" Heath asked.

"Like a baby." With a wide smile, Dr. Johnson turned to gaze out of the side window. "Oh, look at that—back at Chapel Cove already."

"Safe and sound." Heath slowed the truck to a stop at the crossing where the open road met their home town. "So, Doc. Left or right? Home or office?"

"Left, son. I need to get to the clinic." The doctor chuckled. "Besides, my car is parked there."

Of course it was. Heath had totally forgotten that the doctor had followed the ambulance to the clinic yesterday.

Yesterday… Could that have been only twenty-two hours ago? Felt like a lifetime since he was on the carpet in the aisle, trying to save Ivy's life. So much had happened. So many emotions ranging from fear and despair to hopes and dreams.

When Heath parked outside the clinic, Dr. Johnson turned to him. "Won't you come in for a minute? I see the new doctor is here already—he's certainly off to a good start—and I'd like to introduce you to him."

"Sure." Heath opened the door and clambered out. He held his hand to Reese. "You coming?"

"Yes. I'd like to meet the new doctor too, seeing as I'll be hanging around Chapel Cove for the foreseeable future."

As they entered, a tall, brown-haired gent dressed in a white coat stood with his back to the door. He was chatting to the receptionist, Marylin. Not that Marylin was *just* the receptionist, according to Aunt Ivy who had been friends with Marylin for years. No, she was that and much, much more. She made appointments for patients, kept the clinic's books, and made sure that Dr. Johnson's coffee cup and water jug were always filled.

The white-coated gent turned, and Heath's eyes widened. They both rushed forward.

"Hudson! What are— Are *you* the new doctor? Why didn't you tell me?" Heath whirled around to Dr. Johnson. "Why didn't *you* tell me?"

Dr. Johnson laughed. "Dr. Brock wanted me to keep it a surprise."

"Well, mission accomplished." Heath beamed and wrapped his younger sibling in a bear hug, slapping his back. "Man, it's good to see you. I can't believe you're going to be the other doctor in town."

"It's good to see you too, brother."

With a last squeeze, Hudson took a step back. He twisted toward Reese, standing to one side. "And who is this beautiful lady?" He narrowed his eyes and moved closer. A grin stretched across his face. "No way... Clarise Aylward? Is that really you?"

"It's really me. Rough night." Reese flung her arms around Hudson and hugged him. "So you made it to become a doctor. I always knew you'd go far."

"And you made it to supermodel, just as you dreamed about all those years ago."

Hudson's voice faded to white noise as doubt dug its talons into Heath's heart. What had Reese thought about him? That he'd never amount to much? Why not? He would've thought that of his twenty-year old self. But what about now? Did Reese think she'd been right all along? The loser youth pastor still living on the beach in the same aging camper...

If she only knew there was so much more to this youth pastor than met the eye, than what he chose to reveal to the world.

And he would choose to reveal everything to her when the time was right.

Hudson's voice filtered into Heath's consciousness, drawing him from his reverie.

"...really good. Heath showed me some fashion magazines where you were the cover model."

"Heath has fashion magazines with me in?" Reese's gaze

shifted to him.

Heath shrugged. "Guilty as charged. I was proud of you. And I wanted to follow your career."

Even though it was painful.

Heath shifted his focus to Hudson and changed the subject. "So little brother, I'm intrigued. The world was your oyster... Why Chapel Cove?"

"It's home. I've always loved it here. When I saw Dr. Johnson advertising for a partner in the clinic, I jumped at the opportunity."

A loud guffaw came from behind them where the doctor had been conversing with Marylin. "You were the only one who jumped, Dr. Brock. Seems not many men, or women, are interested in being a small town doctor."

Fingers to his chin, Hudson rubbed his jaw in thought. "Hmm, so *that's* how I landed this opportunity of a lifetime."

"Not at all," Dr. Johnson replied. "I couldn't believe God had looked down on me with such favor when I received your CV and qualifications. Chapel Cove and I are honored to have such a distinguished and qualified doctor, and surgeon, serving us."

"Hear, hear." Reese clapped her hands in delight.

Taking Hudson by the elbow, Heath whispered to him, "Can I have a quick word with you in private?"

Hudson nodded. "Excuse us for a moment. Family business..."

They strode across to the far wall, out of earshot.

"Do you have a place to stay?" Heath asked.

Hudson's shoulders shook with a chuckle. "Why? Are you offering to let me bunk down with you in your camper? You're still staying on the beach, I presume? At least you were the last time I visited. Can't believe that was almost two years ago. Oh my, that was the most cramped ten days of my life. I almost checked into a B&B."

"At least my place has the best view in town." Heath smacked

Hudson's arm. "C'mon, admit it."

"Yes, you're right—can't beat the view. Anyway, thanks for the offer, but I'm booked into the bed and breakfast just across the bridge for the next month. No view, but the food is good—*and* they provide dinners. Plus it's not far from the clinic."

A guffaw tumbled from Heath's mouth. "Nothing is far from anything in Chapel Cove. But, jokes aside, Uncle Trafford's place is vacant. You're welcome to crash there if you want. View's good too, but you already know that."

"You mean, *your* place. Uncle Trafford left it all to you, not that I blame him—you were the only one always there for him. I was too busy with football, which did give me my college scholarship, and Hunter…well, he was too busy getting up to all kinds of shenanigans. I'm glad you got the RV and trailer parks and Uncle Trafford's home. I just don't understand why you persist in staying in that old camper instead of the house. It's a beautiful old place with loads of character and space! Especially after the mods Uncle Trafford undertook after buying the house."

Memories, that's why. The camper held the most special and intimate memories of Reese. And the house…well it mostly held memories of Uncle Trafford's suffering and death.

Heath pushed that last remembrance away. "Because the house is good income in the summer months."

"Handy. I guess a youth pastor's salary in a small town doesn't stretch that far, huh? But you do have the income from the RV and trailer parks too. Isn't that sufficient?"

Heath cracked a grin then placed a finger to his lips. "Shh, people will think I'm rolling in money."

"And then there's that other thing…" Hudson said, a twinkle in his eye.

Heath shook his head to dissuade Hudson from saying anything further. Walls have ears, so they say.

Hudson pretended to zip his lip which brought a relieved sigh from Heath. And a smile. He was going to enjoy having his younger brother around. They'd always gotten along well.

Unzipping his lips again, Hudson said, "I'll definitely bear your offer in mind, although I will get a real estate agent to start looking into available property for me to purchase. I want to set down roots here, Heath, find a wife, start a family, so if I did take you up on *your* house, it would only be short term. I'd be out before your summer bookings start."

"I don't have any reservations yet." Heath shrugged. "Strange."

Hudson's eyebrow quirked. "Indeed. Well, if you hear of anything good on the market, let me know, okay?"

"I definitely will."

Nudging Heath, Hudson tipped his head in Reese's direction. "So, what's with you and Reese? You back together again?"

If only.

Heath shot Reese a glance and his heart thumped. She was deep in conversation with Dr. Johnson and Marylin. He shook his head. "Not yet. I only saw her for the first time on Saturday since she left Chapel Cove in search of fame and fortune."

"Well, she certainly found that all right." Hudson's eyes narrowed. "Wait a minute. What do you mean 'not yet'? Does that mean you plan on trying to win her back? Is she even here to stay? I don't want to see you getting heartbroken again. The last time cost you a life of solitude."

Heath grinned. "Hah, says the man who's nearing forty and still single too."

"Well, I do have plans to remedy that soon."

Heath's brows shot up. What was his little brother not telling him? "Does that mean you have someone in mind?"

"Not the faintest idea. But God knows. And I just have the feeling that He's going to have her stumble into my life very soon."

Heath hoped that both he and Hudson would have their prayers answered.

Hudson clasped Heath's arm. "Is that how you feel…about Reese?"

"I believe she's back to stay. And I guess only time will tell whether or not I can win her heart again. But I'm certainly praying that I can."

After leaving the clinic, Heath opened the truck's passenger door and Reese slid inside once again. He shut the door behind her then hurried around to the driver's side, his emotions riding high. Alone at last, he could finally ask her if she'd go out on a date with him.

"Well, that was a surprise," she said as Heath clambered in behind the wheel. "Hudson the new doctor in town… Who would've guessed? You must be so excited to have your brother back in Chapel Cove."

"A total surprise for sure. I had absolutely no idea he was planning this. And yes, I'm thrilled that Hudson is back. It's been lonely without family around."

"Your father? Did he move away?"

Heath shook his head, wishing he didn't have to revisit this memory. But Reese needed to get to know him again, morsel by morsel whether bitter or sweet.

"My dad died not long after I started Bible college in Portland. He finally drank himself to death. Uncle Trafford found him during his morning rounds of the trailer park." Heath heaved a sigh and clamped his fingers around the steering wheel. "I think the loneliness got to him. Maybe if I'd never left—"

"Don't!" Reese's hand slid over his. "Don't do that to yourself.

You followed your heart, the plan God had for your life. It won't help you to dwell on what-ifs."

Is that how she'd managed to live with her own decisions to leave Chapel Cove, to leave him?—by not dwelling on what could have been between them if she'd stayed?

Heath shuddered to think what could have happened to him had he not found God. He could very well have suffered the same fate as his father. Dad never got over Mom leaving them. Sometimes he wondered whether his father had died as a result of the liquor or a broken heart.

They'd never heard from their mother again. She could be dead for all he knew. He'd never understand how a mother could desert her children. Then again, she had never been a very good mother…it was as if she hadn't wanted children. Although Chapel Cove seemed to have been the nail in the coffin for his parents' turbulent marriage—Mom leaving after merely a month—he'd probably never know the reason why she had left and never looked back. The last words he'd heard her speak before the front door of their trailer had slammed and she'd disappeared into the night were angry words spoken to their father.

"I'll not become trailer trash. I'm far better than the existence you've subjected me to."

Not wishing to dwell on his father's fate, or the void his mother had left in their lives—some mother was better than no mother, wasn't it?—Heath continued, "Hudson was almost finished with med school when I moved to Portland. And Hunter had taken off to sunny California years before, shortly after his first stint in jail in—"

"Hunter served time?" Reese's brows arched.

"Still is. Managed to keep out of trouble for a number of years—or dodge the law—but his sins finally caught up with him. Currently he's serving out a ten year sentence in LA. He comes up for parole in a few months. I'm hoping this time he'll get out."

"How long has he been in for?"

"Nearly eight years."

Reese's eyes widened. "Wow, that's a long time. I'm sorry his life went in the wrong direction."

"Me too, but I have hope and faith that this time things will be different. When I visited him last week, he actually had some spiritual questions. And as I was leaving, he asked me to pray for him and not to give up."

"That does sound promising. I hope he changes, for your sake and Hudson's."

So did Heath. If Hunter accepted the offer he planned to make regarding the RV and trailer parks, perhaps his brother wouldn't have a reason to go back to a life of crime.

Heath started the engine. Twisting his head to peer out the rear window, he backed out of the parking space. As he did, an idea hit him. He didn't want his time with Reese to end. And she must surely be famished.

He turned to her. "Would you like to go for breakfast? There's a neat little place on the boardwalk overlooking the ocean that serves the best pancakes this side of the west coast. Drizzled with warm maple syrup, crisp fried bacon on the side." Heath licked his lips for effect. He got the impression yesterday that Reese still loved food as much as she had as a teen, so he hoped the way to her heart might be through her stomach. As it supposedly was for a man.

She remained silent for a while, and his pulse beat faster and harder with each passing second.

Please, say yes.

Finally, Reese raised her gaze to meet his expectant one. "Tempting as that sounds, I–I'm not sure it would be a good idea. Not now, at least. I need time."

CHAPTER TEN

REESE BOUNCED out of bed with a purpose she hadn't felt in a long time and hurried to get dressed. Comfy sweat pants and a loose T-shirt should do the trick. A sweatshirt to ward off the cold outside.

As she put on her clothes, her mind drifted to yesterday and the things she should have done.

After Heath had dropped her off at home, the day had passed at a snail's pace. She'd spent most of her time regretting turning down his offer of breakfast, her mind dwelling on how good those pancakes would've tasted.

Not only did she bemoan the fact that she had missed out on a scrumptious meal, but she also regretted not spending extra time with Heath. She *had* to take things slowly with him though. After all, she was only recently divorced, and the last thing she wanted was a rebound relationship with no lasting feelings involved. She had no desire to hurt Heath again. With butterflies swirling in her tummy every time her skin brushed against his, not to mention the way her heart had somersaulted at that kiss last night, she had to be sure it wasn't just some kind of infatuation or purely a physical attraction. Worse, a last-ditch attempt to relive her youth before she turned the big four-oh.

So when Kristina called early this morning suggesting they go over to Aunt Ivy's bookshop to help Nai reorganize a bedroom for her aunt that didn't involve climbing a staircase, Reese jumped at the invitation. True to form, Nai had been too stubborn and independent to ask for help, her text last night only stating that she'd arrived back in Chapel Cove, was tired from the long day and heading straight for bed. She promised to call in the morning to update Reese and Kristina on Aunt Ivy.

Frankly, Reese was surprised that her friend was back in Chapel Cove at all. She'd been certain Nai would find a hotel in Portland near the hospital and stay until Aunt Ivy was discharged. But knowing Aunt Ivy, she had probably been the one to insist that Nai come back to look after her bookstore and whatever rescue pets she currently owned.

When Reese texted Nai back, asking when they would see her—and likely Kristina had sent a similar message—she'd replied as soon as she'd fixed up the house for Aunt Ivy. A day or two at the most.

Reese sent one final text, offering to come over in the morning to help, but Nai never replied, even though Reese could see that she'd read the text.

Kristina suggested she and Reese meet at the bookshop around nine a.m. Reese couldn't wait, relishing the opportunity to do something different other than the boring routine that had become her sad and sorry life since she'd returned to Chapel Cove over seven weeks ago.

Plus, the distraction would be welcome. She needed to fill her mind with something other than thoughts of Heath.

She'd always loved the idea that Aunt Ivy lived above the bookshop, a place Reese hadn't set foot inside in years—but only because she hadn't been in Chapel Cove in years. Even when she had come home, the visits had been so brief. That's why she hadn't given it a thought yesterday that Aunt Ivy might have a problem recovering from her heart attack in her own home.

After tying her hair in a ponytail, Reese skipped downstairs and burst into the kitchen.

Mom stood beside the stove. She glanced up. "Morning, Reese."

Reese squealed and rushed forward. "Are those pancakes you're making?"

Her mother's mouth curved upward. "What do you think? Yesterday, you threw out so many hints about being in the mood for pancakes, I wasn't about to risk a replay today."

Reese kissed her mother's cheek then sneaked one of the pancakes from the plate.

Mom swatted her hand. "Hey, young lady…"

Shooting her mother a cheeky look, Reese flounced away and plopped herself down at the table. She grabbed the maple syrup and drizzled the sweet nectar over the pancake. "All this needs now is some bacon on the side."

Mom opened the oven and the aroma of bacon crisping under the grill wafted toward Reese. Reese breathed in the delicious smell. "Mom, you're the best. Can I stay here forever?"

Hands immediately on her hips, Mom turned back to face Reese. "No, Reese. This was not a decision your father and I took lightly. We gave it a lot of thought. Our ultimatum stands, and just a reminder, the clock is ticking."

Mom's face softened, her hands relaxing at her sides. "Believe me, sweetheart, we're doing this for your own good, even though it might not feel like that to you right now."

Reese's bottom lip protruded with an excessive pout.

"Instead of sitting there sulking, young lady, why don't you go call your father for breakfast. He's outside tinkering in the garage." Mom's fingers waved toward the back door.

Hmm. Maybe if she toed the line, made herself indispensable, her parents would have a change of heart and keep her around longer.

"Sure, no problem." She pushed to her feet then flounced out the back door and around the house.

Deep inside the garage, Dad was busy working on something.

"Morning, Dad."

Hearing Reese, he dropped a wrench. It clanged on the concrete floor as he pivoted. "Oh... Oh no, you shouldn't be in here." His shoulders rose then slumped as he inhaled then exhaled. "But, seeing as you are..."

He stepped to the side, and Reese clamped a hand to her mouth, excitement bubbling up inside of her. "I–is that my old bicycle? From high school?"

Dad beamed. "It is. Although it's had a thorough service and cleaning. The frame has even been repainted black." He patted the front tire. "Practically brand new, it is."

"Oh, Dad." Reese flung her arms around her father's neck. "I can't believe you did that." This was the ideal solution for now for her transport problems. She couldn't borrow her parents' car to get around—they needed it. Plus, navigating on two wheels was probably just what her legs and thighs required. She couldn't believe she hadn't thought of buying a bicycle. Her mind had been so fixed on how she was going to afford a car. Probably the result of years of owning fancy wheels, or being chauffeured around. At least she now had one less thing to budget for; she had a perfectly good set of wheels right here.

Oh, wouldn't Lloyd get a sadistic kick out of this.

Pfft. Who cared what he thought? The sooner she forgot he ever existed, the better.

"I figured you'd need some mode of transport soon. I remember how much you loved riding your bike around town, to your friends' houses, the beach, the chapel... I hope this helps in the interim. Until you get back on your feet again." Dad laid a gentle hand on her shoulder. "And you will."

"Thanks, Dad. It does. Have you finished refurbishing the bike?"

Dad smiled. "If I'd had another ten minutes..."

Reese linked her arm in his. "How about we eat breakfast before it spoils, then when I'm gathering my stuff, you can get your ten minutes. Kristina and I are helping Nai prepare a room downstairs at the bookshop for Aunt Ivy. This'll be the perfect time to take it for a test run."

And maybe when they were done at the bookshop, she could take the long way home—via the boardwalk and the beach.

Butterflies fluttered in Reese's stomach as the old, two-story Victorian house with its moss-green timber cladding loomed in front of her. As a child, she'd thought it was such a quirky place to have a bookshop, complete with café serving the most delicious coffee and cakes. Now she found it simply beautiful.

Everyone in Chapel Cove knew and loved Aunt Ivy's bookshop, Ivy's on Spruce. Reese was no exception.

She leaned her bike against the wooden banister then bounded up the steps leading to the front door. She could barely wait to see her old friends again. It had been way too many years since they'd all been together at the same time. Yes, she'd seen Kristina and Nai at least once every other year—give or take—after they'd all left Chapel Cove, but always only one or the other. Them being together in one place at the same time was like she'd really come home.

And wouldn't Nai be surprised to see her and Kristina. Speaking of whom, where was their youngest friend? No point in waiting for her; she might as well go inside.

Before Reese could even ring the bell, the door flew open. Without a word, Nai wrapped Reese in her embrace. Beside them, a beige, wiry-haired mutt yapped. Must be one of Aunt Ivy's rescues. No doubt there'd be more—perhaps another dog or two, a bird, or a cat. Knowing Aunt Ivy, there could even be a flying squirrel.

"Heinz! Shush!" Nai shouted.

From behind them, Kristina's enthusiastic scream split through the air before she lunged into the group hug. "The trio's back together again!" she squealed.

Well, that explained things. She'd arrived early.

"For a while, at least." Nai clamped her hands around Reese's cheeks, then Kristina's, and grinned. "You girls... I should've known to keep silent about needing to rearrange the house. But oh my, it's so good to see you both again. And after one look at Aunt Ivy's downstairs apartment, I'm *really* glad you're here."

A warm fuzziness circled in Reese's tummy, cocooning those butterflies. Her friends loved her. Always had. Always would. At least she had that. It felt so good to be loved by someone other than her parents. Although, at the moment, Mom and Dad had a rather peculiar way of showing their love.

Pushing away the thoughts of having to find work and somewhere to stay, she returned Nai's smile. "It's good to see you too. It's been way too long. I only wish it was under better circumstances. How is Aunt Ivy recovering?"

Nai's dark brows knit together behind her oversized glasses. "Not that great." She swallowed hard, and Reese was certain that her usually controlled friend was stifling a sob. In the few seconds before Nai released a heavy sigh, Reese caught a glimpse of the uncertain young girl her friend had once been.

"That's why we have a lot to do today," Nai continued. "We need to clear out the downstairs apartment and prepare it for Aunt Ivy—it'll be a while before she'll be able to climb the stairs to her bedroom again."

Lowering her gaze for a moment, Nai nervously wound the end of her T-shirt around her fingers. "H–her heart…it's not working as well as it should, suffered some muscle damage."

Reese's eyes stung and her vision blurred. Poor Aunt Ivy. Life was so uncertain. It could change in an instant.

Her thoughts turned to Heath. Maybe she'd go by his camper after they finished up here today. Aunt Ivy's condition made her realize that nobody is guaranteed tomorrow.

And she was no exception.

The day had gone by in a blur of hard work and sweet memories, and Reese could barely believe the clock had just struck seven when she walked out the bookshop's door. She'd still get home way before the sun set, but just in time for dinner. Good, because she was hungry.

Exhausted, her muscles aching, Reese hopped on her bike and waved goodbye to her friends. She pedaled down the short path leading away from Aunt Ivy's. "See you Saturday afternoon. Nai, we'll celebrate your birthday in style, I promise."

Nai shouted back, "Coffee and cake and more catching up right here at the bookshop with my besties is good enough for me."

Right... So not going to happen. That pancake shop had a table with their name on it for Saturday afternoon. At least, it would have soon—once she'd chatted to Kristina about her idea and then spoken to Dr. Johnson. Besides, it seemed as if Cupid needed a little help kick-starting the oldies' romance, and this was the perfect way to get Nai out of the house, and the good doctor in.

Being back in that tiny one-roomed apartment behind the bookshop had been such a nostalgic journey. Sporting its own kitchenette and half bath with a shower, the mother-in-law's apartment had been Nai's home from the age of sixteen until she left Chapel Cove. Moving to Aunt Ivy's and getting away from her mother had been the best thing to happen to her friend, even though the transition hadn't been without drama from Nai's mother.

Old photos and high school pennants still covered the faded pink walls. Reminiscing on each one, they'd merely dusted them off, leaving them in place.

Aunt Ivy's two shop assistants, throwbacks from the hippie era, managed the bookshop and café for the day. Well, Violet, the older one a throwback with her purple clothes and purple streak in her white hair. Younger Fern just a wannabe hippie and about as eccentric as Violet.

With them manning the business, Reese, Nai and Kristina were free to slog boxes of books and store supplies from the apartment to a spare room upstairs—one that didn't seem to have a problem with a leaking roof. Goodness, the woman didn't only sell books, she hoarded them too.

With each heavy box, the thought never left Reese that they'd have to do this again in reverse in the not too distant future. Once Aunt Ivy was well enough to navigate the stairs to her bedroom, she'd certainly want things returned to normal. And that would mean putting everything back into "storage". But perhaps then, Nai would accept the help offered from tall, dark strangers who came knocking at her door after hearing about her aunt.

Not that Mateo was a stranger.

As a teen, Nai had always had a crush on the boy. And although rivals in the chess club who constantly competed to come top of the math class, Nai and Mateo had also been friends. Such a pity they'd never managed to break out of that friends' zone because they did make a cute couple. Reese was certain that Mateo would've made Nai happy, and saved her from becoming a bachelorette.

If only… Nai could've spared herself a lifetime of devoting herself to her career.

Hah, she was a fine one to talk. Had trophies been given out for putting one's career above love, Reese would've had the biggest, shiniest cup there ever was.

Her thoughts shifted to Heath. She had chosen the fashion world over him. Suddenly, more than anything, she regretted that decision.

Instinctively, she turned her bicycle left onto Hemlock Avenue. It would only take a few minutes to cycle to the beach. And Heath's camper.

Her heart pounded at the thought of seeing him again. Maybe she should throw caution to the wind and let him know how he still made her feel. There was no denying that she wanted to explore whether, after all these years, they could make it work.

She shot a selfish prayer heavenward that he'd be home.

After a hectic day at work, counseling three young people in the congregation as well as preparing for youth church on Sunday, Heath pulled his truck to a stop outside his camper.

Inside his small home, he cracked open a pop, craving the energy the sugar rush would bring. He took a long drink, then set the can down on the counter and flopped onto his bed. The walls of the camper squeezed.

Whoa, in all the years of living here, he'd never felt this way. Was it perhaps time to follow Hudson's example and find a wife, settle down to married life? Especially now that Reese was back in town and single? This was the first time he'd entertained marriage in over two decades. With Reese at his side, Uncle Trafford's house wouldn't feel as big and empty.

He shot upright, shaking his head. What a ridiculous notion. Reese had turned down a simple breakfast request; imagine what she'd do with a proposal.

He had to be cautious not to move too fast with her.

Then again, he needed to be equally careful not to repeat the mistakes of the past and take too long to let her know that he was still madly in love with her.

Had never stopped loving her.

Desperate for air, Heath downed the rest of his drink, then grabbed his camera and truck keys. It was barely past seven. At least fifty minutes before the sun would set and the Oregon skies would explode into a canvas of orange, pink, and blue. And he knew exactly where to get the perfect shot—up at the old chapel on the cove.

The farther down Wharf Road Reese pedaled, the harder her heart thwacked against her ribs. Not from exhaustion either. She'd only cycled a quarter mile from Aunty Ivy's, barely far enough to break a sweat.

Up ahead, the trees surrounding the RV park drew closer, their leafy boughs offering some privacy from the roads of Chapel Cove. Reese could just make out Heath's camper.

Almost there.

Taking care, she navigated the narrow path between the trees, soon arriving at her destination. Her heart sank. Heath's truck was nowhere in sight. Could he have loaned it to Hudson? A girl could hope.

Reese leaned her bike against a tree then strode to the door of the camper. Raising her hand, she tapped her knuckles against the aluminum door. "Heath, are you there?"

Only silence returned her call.

Surely he couldn't still be at work? It was after seven. Was it youth night at the church? Or had he maybe just had as tiring a day as she and dozed off.

She tried once more.

Still nothing.

Either he was a deep sleeper, or the man wasn't home. Or just didn't want to open.

Reese's breath hitched. What if he was out on a date with someone? Oh why hadn't she taken him up on his breakfast offer yesterday?

On the other hand, what if this was the worst idea she'd ever come up with? Maybe they were just not meant for each other, and Heath not being here was God's way of protecting her from making another big mistake with him.

And maybe God simply wasn't interested in hearing her prayers—not that He'd listened in a very long time. Seemed her prayer for Heath to be home was yet another in a long line of unanswered ones.

But she would give God the benefit of the doubt for a little while longer, give Him a tad more time to answer her simple prayer.

Leaving her bike parked, she strode closer to the water's edge and plopped herself down on the dry sand. She sent a quick text to her mom to let her know she'd be late. No point in wasting a perfectly good sunset. If Heath wasn't home by the time it was dark, she'd take that as a sign and pedal back home as fast as she could, putting Heath Brock and this near mistake behind her forever.

CHAPTER ELEVEN

HEATH HAD been right. The Pancake Shoppe on the boardwalk did serve the best pancakes this side of the west coast. Granted, she hadn't opted for his suggestion of drizzling them with warm maple syrup, crisp fried bacon on the side—it was way too late in the day for that, and besides, Mom had made that for breakfast merely four days ago—but her choice of a Dutch pancake was spot on. The vanilla-scented, wood-fired Bismarck—more soufflé-like than a pancake—topped with roasted pears and honey and sprinkled with powdered sugar, was a custardy treat, and the perfect way to spend the Saturday afternoon celebrating Nai's birthday.

Nai had driven to Portland that morning to fetch her aunt who was finally discharged from hospital.

Dr. Johnson had jumped at the opportunity to watch over Aunt Ivy while the girls relaxed for a few hours together. In fact, he'd insisted they take their time. Reese hoped that he'd make the most of the hours they were away. Who knew, maybe by the time they returned, the good doctor would at last have declared his undying love to Aunt Ivy.

Images of the day and night spent with Dr. Johnson and Heath in Portland flashed through her mind.

And the kisses she and Heath had shared in a moment of weakness.

Ugh, would thoughts of the man hound her forever? Hadn't she vowed on Tuesday night that she was done with Heath Brock? The sun had set, he hadn't returned, and she'd cycled home in the dark, disappointed and feeling the fool but taking it as a sign that they were never meant to be. How had she allowed her emotions to get the better of her yet again?

She'd chalk up her impulsive actions to not thinking straight from sheer exhaustion. That's all.

Forking another mouthful between her lips, Reese savored the sweet taste. Around the table, silence reigned as the girls enjoyed their sweet treats—Kristina the blueberry pancakes smothered with cream and Nai the "healthier" option of lemon ricotta. At least, that's the way they'd sold it to Nai who'd seemed reluctant to indulge, even though it was her birthday and they were celebrating. And who could blame her? She'd trimmed down so much, she probably didn't want to pick up the pounds she'd shed—although Nai would never admit to that.

Reese washed the pancake down with a swig of coffee and turned to Nai. "I can't believe how much weight you've lost since the last time I saw you in Austin."

Nai set her fork down on her plate and wiped her mouth with the white, linen napkin. "Well, that was almost two years ago, and a stressful job will do that to a person."

Smiling, Reese nodded. "Tell me about it. I'm probably going to get as fat as a pregnant pig now that I'm back in Chapel Cove. No job, no stress," she joked, although the thought that time was ticking by fast to find work and an apartment weighed heavily on her mind. But her friends didn't need to know about that. Not yet. They'd only try to resolve her situation, and she had to do this on her own. She had to prove to her parents that she could do it.

Maybe, in a way, she was just as stubborn as Nai.

If only Aunt Ivy hadn't suffered a heart attack, she could've asked to rent the mother-in-law apartment at the bookshop. But that option was out of the question now, at least for the foreseeable future.

"You, fat? Never," Kristina said before helping herself to another piece of blueberry deliciousness.

Nai leaned forward. "So, tell us everything about your day together with Heath. You were really evasive about it on Tuesday but you can't keep us in the dark forever."

Reese rolled her eyes and gazed out of the window. On the beach nearby, waves broke, rolling up the sandy shore. As always, seagulls drifted in the wind, or lined the railing that edged the boardwalk. "Nothing to tell. The Brock ship sailed a long time ago. You know that."

Nai lifted one shoulder in a shrug then eased back in her chair. "True. But there are no rules that state a ship can never return to the same harbor. Maybe this time more than one person will drop anchor and stay."

Standing behind the pulpit at Chapel Cove Community Church, Heath's gaze roamed the sanctuary. Don had asked him to present the progress report he was supposed to give last Sunday morning on his work with the youth.

Near the back of the church, he spotted that familiar head of strawberry-blond, flanked on one side by long dark hair and a shorter, brown bob on the other. Just as he'd seen so many times as the three friends grew up—at school, in the streets, on the beach, riding their bikes.

So, all the girls were back in town. Heath couldn't help but wonder what advice Reese's best friends were giving her concerning him.

Run a million miles.

Stay away.

You've only just escaped from one bad marriage; don't get sucked into another.

He shoved aside the negative thoughts. They had no reason to think that of him. They didn't know him. Not anymore. Besides, they'd always gotten along as teens—why would things change now? They knew how distraught he'd been at the news that Reese had skipped town to follow her dreams in New York. They knew how he'd felt about their friend. But what they didn't know was how he *still* felt about her.

Filling his lungs, he gripped the sides of the pulpit, leaned forward and smiled. "Morning, Church."

"Morning, Pastor Heath" rumbled back, like a Mexican wave.

Forcing himself to concentrate on the task at hand, Heath delivered a flawless talk on his work with the teens of Chapel Cove. He thanked the church for the opportunity to update them on his ministry then took his seat again.

Concentrating on Don's sermon was nothing short of challenging. All Heath could think about during the next thirty minutes was how much space he would need to give Reese and what he could do to win her heart. If only she could've watched that spectacular sunset with him on Tuesday. So romantic, guaranteed to have won her heart. Hopefully one day soon he'd be able to enjoy one with her. In fact, he prayed they'd be able to share the rest of their sunsets together.

He knew what he had to do. He was done waiting for Reese. He'd waited twenty-two long years for her. No more. He was going to pull out all the stops to get his girl.

As soon as the last hymn was sung and the benediction prayed, Heath wove between congregants toward the back rows where he'd seen Reese and her friends seated. He'd ask Reese out again—maybe this time she'd say yes. Hopefully she'd missed him this past week as much as he'd missed her.

Spotting Reese fawning all over some well-built guy on crutches, he stopped. Probably not the best time to ask her on a date.

The guy turned to peer over his shoulder.

Wait a minute—that was Kristina's twin brother, Roman.

Heath's heart plummeted, leaving a hollow ache in its wake. Did Reese have a thing for him, too, when they were growing up?

Seeing Heath heading her way, Reese smiled at Roman. She eased past Kristina and gently touched Roman's shoulder, allowing her hand to brush down his arm. Maybe that would encourage Mr. Brock to stay away from her.

"Roman, it's good to see you again." With Kristina and her brother arriving late for church, none of them had yet had a chance to speak. She leaned closer to give him a hug, one he couldn't return thanks to his crutches.

When she released him, Roman's brows raised in surprise and he grinned. "Likewise."

Reese lifted her gaze in time to see Heath's set jaw before he turned on his heel and marched back the way he came. She didn't know whether to feel relieved or disappointed. Had she just dodged a bullet, or missed an opportunity? The more logical question was, had Heath even been on his way to her?

With Heath gone, Reese whirled back to Kristina and wrapped her in a hug too. She didn't want Roman to get the wrong impression about her brief flirtation. "Kris, I'm glad you made it."

"Me too," Kristina said. "That was a great sermon—just what I needed to hear in order to start forgiving Cullen."

Reese had also been touched by the pastor's words from the book of Romans on vengeance and God's love, but it might take her a little longer to even think about forgiving Lloyd. She had lost everything because of him.

As for Heath, she had forgiven him a long time ago, and herself, but going down that road again?—wasn't that what God had prevented by not letting Heath be home the night she'd swung by his place?

"I didn't expect to see you in church, Nai." Kristina's voice drew Reese from memory lane. "Who's looking after Aunt Ivy?"

"Dr. Johnson. After I got home last night—and by the way girls, thank you so much for spoiling me on my birthday yesterday—he insisted on coming back this morning so I could go to church and give God thanks for saving Aunt Ivy's life. There was no reasoning with him that I'd already done so. I figured I might as well humor the man and give him the time with my aunt. She does seem to enjoy his company. He's good for her, I think."

"He is." Reese had seen it for herself.

She released a heavy sigh. If only there was someone who was good for Reese Aylward.

After church, Mom prepared a wonderful lunch of roast chicken, mashed potatoes, gravy, green beans, and carrots. As tasty as the meal was, Reese picked at her food. She couldn't shrug off the sick feeling that she'd made a big mistake inside the church when she deliberately hugged Roman, knowing Heath would see. She'd wanted to dissuade the man—well, mission accomplished. The remaining time Reese was in the sanctuary, she'd spotted Heath twice, conversing with one of the congregation. Whatever he was on his way to talk to her about—*if* he'd been on his way to talk to her—he'd obviously had second thoughts.

Mom's hand clasped around Reese's, startling her. "Reese, dear, is everything all right? You've barely touched your food, and that's so unlike you."

Reese shook her head. She needed to snap out of this funk.

"I'm fine, Mom. Just thinking about Aunt Ivy, that's all. I didn't expect to see her so weak when I saw her yesterday." Well, at least part of what she'd said was true.

"Just give her time, sweetheart. She's been through quite an ordeal, and it's only been a week." Mom's chair scraped against the kitchen floor as she eased out of it. "In the meantime, I have something that might cheer you up. I'll be back in a second."

She hurried from the kitchen, her footsteps soon pounding the stairs as she rushed to the second floor.

Dad raised his shoulders and hands in ignorance. "I promise I have absolutely no idea what she's up to."

Soon Mom returned, waving a newspaper. "I went through this with a fine toothcomb yesterday. There are some wonderful jobs available, as well as a few prospective places to stay."

Goodness, but her mother seemed determined to get her out of the house. Reese just couldn't understand why. She'd thought after leaving home at such a tender age, her parents would be only too happy to have her back home for good. But quite the opposite was the case, it seemed.

Annoyed, she snatched the paper from her mother. Might as well see if there was anything acceptable there. She glanced at the jobs section first and all the ads circled in red, then rolled her eyes. "Seriously, Mom. Cashier at the post office? Waitress at Tía Irma's Mexican restaurant?"

"Reese, don't shut yourself off from trying new things. There, what about this one?" Mom pressed her finger to the red circle near the bottom of the page. Clearly she'd memorized the employment opportunities. "Sales clerk at a clothing store. I bet you'd be great at that."

Reese vaulted out of her chair, scrunching the newspaper as she did. A frustrated groan rumbled from her chest, and she stomped out of the kitchen.

Grabbing her mother's windbreaker from the hook at the front door, she fled from the house. She needed breathing room to process this. If the jobs her mother had chosen were so...distasteful...she could only imagine what kind of accommodation she had circled with that wicked red pen. Didn't Mom realize she didn't just need a job? She needed a purpose, a passion, a calling. Something she was born to do, besides being a model—those days were over now. Yes, if push came to shove she probably could handle selling clothes for a while, but it wasn't what she could see herself doing for the next twenty-five years until retirement.

Twenty-five years? She wanted to cry. She was getting old. And in merely a day, she'd tip the scales to the rest of her life being downhill. She should find the nearest cliff and jump. What was the purpose of her life anyway?

Reese hurried to the garage to grab her bike, thankful she'd changed into her running gear after church. Couldn't imagine trying to pedal in those high-heeled boots. Not to mention the tight jeans.

Throat clogged, tears stinging the backs of her eyes, she hightailed it down the street in the direction of the ocean.

Ignoring the overwhelming desire to rush to the RV park, find Heath, and find refuge in his arms, Reese steered her bicycle toward the boardwalk. Once there, she propped the bike against the railings and ran down the long jetty. Except for one or two people here and there, the boardwalk and jetty were deserted, the colder weather keeping people away or inside the restaurants dotted down the promenade—pity it did nothing for the seagulls who squawked and hovered overhead as they always did, hoping to score some free food. Right now, the solitude from humankind suited her. With sobs tearing at her throat, fewer people meant she'd draw less attention. The seagulls she could still deal with.

From the end of the jetty, she gazed out across the ocean, hoping the sight would calm her.

All it managed to do was stir up her anger once more.

God, You are so mighty. You created all of this—the majestic, unfathomable ocean—why then do You seem so set against me? Why have You allowed me to lose everything...my home, my husband, my career? Why are You so cruel? Now, even my parents seem to have turned against me.

You are able to take care of me, Lord, to give me a home and a job that I will love—not some menial one working behind a cash register or serving tables. And yet, You choose to remain ever silent in my life. As You've done for so many years.

Why?

Why?

Holding tightly to the wooden railing, Reese closed her eyes and sank to her knees, tears wetting her cheeks. She released her grip and buried her face in her hands. *I can't do this on my own.*

Strong arms folded around her. Who was behind her, comforting her so sweetly? Then a familiar voice whispered her name, and Reese's heart hammered.

Heath.

CHAPTER TWELVE

"REESE BABY, what's wrong." Heath tightened his hold on Reese praying his embrace would give her the hope she needed for whatever she was going through.

Sobbing, she pressed her palms to her eyes and shook her head.

Could he get her to open up, to confide in him?

He touched her cheek gently with his finger, brushing it over her soft skin. She was cold.

Removing his woolen cap, Heath placed it on Reese's head and tugged it over her ears. Then he took off his scarf and wound it around her neck. What had she been thinking coming out in this cold weather wearing only a thin windbreaker? No hat, no gloves, nothing to protect her neck from the icy breeze.

"There, that'll make you warmer."

Reese sniffed and nodded, whispering a thank you.

"You know you can talk to me, any time. Whatever has upset you like this, I— I want to help, if you'll let me."

She turned to him, her swollen, red eyes fixing on his. "You can't help me, Heath. I made my bed; I must lie in it. This is *my* mess, and I have to find my own way out of it."

Heath drew in a deep breath then exhaled, his mind churning over what to say next. "Don't always be so stubbornly independent, Reese. It's okay to ask for help or to accept it."

She shifted her gaze back out over the ocean in a vacant stare.

He'd spoken boldly and look where it got him. The cold shoulder. Did he dare utter what he felt the Lord prompting him to say next?

He had nothing to lose and everything to gain...with God's help.

Lord, please let her take these words to heart. Please help her open up to me so that I can help her.

"Have you tried taking the problem to the Lord?" he gently asked.

Without looking at him, Reese snapped, "Why? He's no longer interested in me and my problems." Bitterness tainted her voice.

What had made her turn against God so? He could still remember the times when *she'd* been the one to encourage him to take everything to God in prayer—like it was yesterday.

"You're so wrong, Reese. God loves you with an everlasting love. Just because He might answer your prayers differently than what you'd hoped, doesn't mean that He's turned His back on you. He has said that He will never leave us or forsake us. We never have to be afraid or discouraged—He's told us that over and over in His Word. I've been where you are, and leaning on the Lord has made all the difference. Trust Him, Reese—He'll make something beautiful of your life."

Expecting retaliation at his mini-sermon, Heath was surprised when Reese remained quiet. Hopefully she was processing what he'd said. Refusing to believe otherwise and bracing himself for an onslaught, he gave her silence a while longer.

Finally, Heath let his arm fall from her shoulder and slowly rose. He held out his hand. "Come, let's take a walk."

Reese stared at his outstretched palm for a moment before wrapping her fingers around his wrist and allowing Heath to pull her up.

Back at the start of the jetty, Reese grabbed her bicycle from where it leaned against the railing.

"Here, let me take that for you." Heath took the bike from Reese and pushed it down the boardwalk with one hand. "Is this your old bike from high school?"

The faintest smile brushed her lips. "You remember?"

He nodded.

"Dad surprised me with it on Tuesday after having given it a refurbishing. I didn't even know they still had it." She shrugged. "At least they're wheels *and* a gym all rolled into one. Win-win on the hole in the pocket."

So, it seemed she was having financial problems. Heath was astounded. How was that even possible? She must've amassed a small fortune over the past two decades considering her successes and who her husband had been.

But it could explain her tears.

Heath's camper lay just beyond the boardwalk, down the path through the trees.

"Why don't we leave your bike at my place and stroll further along the beach? It's so peaceful there." He could pick up a thicker jacket for her at the same time.

"That would be nice."

Didn't seem as if she was in any hurry to return home.

They threaded their way through the trees. When they came to his camper, Heath propped the bike against a tall black cottonwood tree then popped into his camper for a second to grab a jacket from the closet. He wrapped it around Reese's shoulders. Taking her hand, he led her onto the beach, surprised she hadn't pulled away from him.

They sauntered down the soft sand in silence, the sound of the ocean filling their ears, sea spray dampening their skin. Neither of them seemed to mind though. It was fresh, it was relaxing, and hopefully it would all be enough to calm Reese and help her to open up to him.

When she took a sharp breath, he swung his attention her way.

"B–before I left New York," Reese began, her voice barely a whisper, gaze remaining fixed on the beach ahead, "I pawned my wedding and engagement rings for a tenth of what they were worth."

"You were *that* mad at your husband?"

She shook her head. "If only. No, because he cheated me *that* badly—not only in breaking our wedding vows to remain faithful to each other and love one another until death parted us, but in swindling me out of my money, my home, my jewelry, my clothes, and railroading my career. Everything I had worked so hard for, gone overnight. Poof. And I no longer had it in me to put up a fight. So I just let it all go.

"I returned to Chapel Cove with barely enough to start over again, and n–now my parents have given me an ultimatum, which they keep reminding me about. At least, my mother does."

Reese paused and turned to Heath. Keeping her eyes downcast, she clasped his hands and trailed her thumbs over his skin. Slowly, she raised her gaze. "I have only three weeks to find myself a job and a place to stay, and I have no idea how I'm going to pull off either."

What she'd gone through—was still going through—was awful.

If only there was something he could do for her.

Heath squeezed her hands.

"Thank you for sharing that with me. I know it couldn't have been easy. And I'm sorry you've been put through so much hardship." He looked deep into her eyes, hoping she could reach inside and feel the reality of God's love. "Honey, God can give you beauty again for your ashes—never let go of that truth."

He cupped her cheek gently. "At least now I know how to effectively pray for you. And I will, Reese. I promise."

She offered him a weak smile. "Thank you, Heath. I appreciate that."

Like a lightning strike, an idea flashed through his mind. He whirled around and headed back the way they'd just come, dragging Reese along with him.

Her soft laugh drifted toward him. "Why have we turned back?"

He stopped and stared at her, his eyes searching hers. "Do you trust me, Reese?"

She tipped her head lightly. "I do."

Heath started to walk again, still holding Reese's hand tightly. "Come, I have something to show you." He had enough time before the evening Youth service.

He'd talk to Hudson after church tonight at their arranged dinner and explain about the change of plans.

Reese's running shoes squeaked on the glossy, Oregon pine floors as she strode into the tastefully furnished white Cape Cod-style home with wrap-around porch. The house was situated on the southern side of Chapel Cove—the more expensive part of the small coastal town. Surrounded by an expanse of green grass and tall trees, the red-roofed, three-story house overlooked the marina on the left. Steep, rugged cliffs bordered the western side of the picket-fenced property called Bliant's Bluff.

Good thing it wasn't Blind Man's Bluff.

She made her way to the open-plan kitchen and stared out of the windows facing the ocean, concern overshadowing her. She turned to Heath. "W–why have you brought me here?"

Stretching his arms sideways, he twirled in a slow circle. "It's all yours, that's why. For as long as you like."

What?

"Hah, I couldn't afford this place for even a month," let alone for as long as she liked, which on first impressions would be forever. "It would render me penniless."

A smile teased the corner of Heath's mouth. "Who said anything about paying? Although, when I said you can stay here for as long as you like, I probably should have added 'for *free*'. The house is standing empty at the moment."

"Right... And whose place would I be crashing, hmm?" Last thing she needed now was to get into trouble with the law on top of everything else that had happened. Quirking an eyebrow, Reese leaned her hip against the dark granite countertop and crossed her arms, waiting for an answer.

A lazy grin slid across Heath's face. Amidst the five o'clock shadow darkening his jaw, his smile seemed whiter. "Mine."

Reese frowned even though she'd spent years avoiding the expression—bad for your complexion Lloyd would chide.

"Y–yours?" If this place *was* Heath's, why did he still live in that tiny camper? This house and view were amazing. No contest whatsoever.

"I inherited it from Uncle Trafford when he passed away," Heath went on to explain, "and rent it out over the summer months. Strangely, I've had no interest this year."

"Yet. There's still a while before the summer holidays."

Heath shook his head. "Bliant's Bluff is normally booked up by now."

Crossing one arm, he tapped a finger to his lips then sucked in a breath. "Here's a crazy thought…maybe there's been no interest because God wanted to keep the house vacant so that I could offer it to you."

Tears stung and Reese swallowed hard. Could it really be that God *was* looking out for her after all?

"I–I couldn't, Heath. You might still get some interest."

Stepping forward, he took her hand and squeezed it. "How about we cross that bridge when, and *if*, we need to? It won't hurt me not to rent the house out this summer. This could be Bliant's Bluff's sabbatical year…you know when the lands are supposed to lay fallow and rest? Technically, it'd be a year early, but I don't think God would mind. Seriously, Reese, I've more than sufficient income from the RV and trailer parks."

Her eyes widened. "Those are yours too?" Goodness, there was much about Heath she didn't know. And she couldn't deny that she wanted to know more, even though she'd tried to convince herself otherwise, that they weren't meant to be.

"They are, though hopefully not for much longer. Once Hunter's out of prison I'm planning to cede both parks to him. Everyone deserves a break in life, and perhaps if he has something of his own, he'll have a reason to stay on the right side of the law this time. Although I have faith he will—I know God is working in his life."

Reese pushed away from the counter. She strolled through the kitchen, opening cupboards and trailing her fingers over the stove, appliances, and counter tops.

Turning, she stared at Heath. "Why don't *you* live here? I mean, the camper…the house…" Her hands weighed up the two options. "I know which place I'd rather choose to put down roots."

Heath raked his hands through his hair, clamping them behind his head for a moment before he spoke. "After moving back to Chapel Cove from Portland to look after my uncle, I lived here with him. It only took four short months for Uncle Trafford to lose his fight with cancer. Once he was gone, I found the place too big for one. Surrounded with too many difficult memories of his illness, I moved back to the camper a month later where there wasn't enough space to feel the emptiness; where I had far more pleasant memories."

Of her?

Heath placed his strong hands on Reese's shoulders. A thrill rippled down her spine at his touch.

"You don't have to give me an answer now, Reese. Just give it some thought. Although I strongly urge you to take the opportunity. Use your time here to figure out what you want to do next in life. Get excited for what lies ahead, and allow God to heal you and lift you up while you're in these beautiful surroundings. There's a very good reason my uncle named this place as he did, for Bliant means healer."

Reese could see herself finding healing here—both emotionally and spiritually.

She would certainly give this a lot of thought, even though there wasn't that much to think about. What better offer could appear on the horizon for her than this?

"Would you like to see the rest of the house? Can't very well expect you to make a decision based on seeing the entrance, kitchen, grounds, and view, now can I?" Heath made his way into the living room.

Reese followed him.

"This was meant to be Uncle Trafford's retirement home," he explained. "I think he'd hoped to share it with Ivy, probably bought when it came on the market because she'd always said how much she loved this house. He first did some renovations, knocked out a few walls to open up the space, put in more modern finishes, polished up those beautiful wooden floors… Unfortunately, only a few months after he'd moved in, he fell ill."

Reese stared out of the windows. "Aunt Ivy would've loved this view, although I wonder if anything would get her to leave her home above her bookshop—even if she claimed to love this house. I certainly couldn't imagine all her rescue animals in this beautiful home, although they'd love the bigger yard."

Reese trailed a hand over the cream-colored couch as she passed it. Pausing, she squeezed the backrest. "Hmm, soft."

"You should sit in it. That couch is way more comfy than you'd think."

Without waiting to be asked twice, she scurried around the oversized armrest and sank into the cushions. "Ooh, that *is* comfortable. I fear if I lived here though, I'd want to spend each waking hour right in this spot, gazing out across the ocean."

"If you became a writer, or ran an online business, you could probably do that." Heath shot her a grin.

"A writer?" She scrunched up her nose, her head giving a tiny shake from side to side. "Can't see that happening. You'd have to ask Hudson how bad my creative compositions were at school."

A low chuckle rumbled from Heath's chest as he rested one knee on the armrest. "It's all about writing what you know, I believe. Maybe you could publish a book about your years as a supermodel—give some star-struck teens wanting to follow the same dream a few pointers and tips."

"Hmm, that is an idea, although I'm not sure it's for me. I'm done with that life."

Reese shifted her gaze to the framed photos on the wall then slowly rose and moved toward the artworks, mesmerized. "Are those…?" She stopped in front of the photos and reached out to touch the glass protecting them. Her finger trailed the cursive signature in the bottom right-hand corner.

Wuthering Heights.

She squealed. "They are! Oh my word, I love this artist—although nobody knows whether the photographer is a man or a woman. His, or her, works are so sought after. I've seen them in more than one renowned New York gallery. In fact, I had two of my own hanging in my penthouse—a birthday present three years ago that cost Lloyd a small fortune. But when he recognized the two photos of the chapel and lighthouse right here at Chapel Cove, he insisted on investing in the works, knowing how much I love this photographer's style—photos taken from, and of, wuthering heights, mostly around our very own, beautiful Oregon."

Mouth downturned, she sighed. "Just another of the special things I had to leave behind."

With the finesse of an art dealer, Reese examined each of the six black and white photos hanging in a neat row. "Wow, the RV and trailer parks must have done well for your uncle all these years for him to be able to afford six of these works."

Heath shrugged. "Perhaps."

Needing to distract her before she guessed, Heath took her by the elbow and led her away. "Should we look at the rest of the house? Then I'll have to drive you home. I'm preaching tonight…Youth service…so I'll need to get changed for that."

His breath hitched. "Hey, Hudson and I are having dinner together after church. You're welcome to join us if you'd like."

"I–I think I'll take a raincheck. I have some big decisions to make, and I need time to think."

"Of course." Heath started toward the wooden staircase. "Oh, there's just one thing. I do need to retain one room in the house. My, um, hobby room off the pantry."

Her brows raised in obvious surprise.

"There's a separate entrance from the backyard, so I wouldn't need to bother you in the least when I use the room. You won't even know I'm there." He'd have to store more clothes at the camper and start using the laundromat in town.

After collecting Reese's bike from where they'd left it beside his camper, Heath deposited her safely back home, disappointed that she'd turned him down for dinner. Hopefully the surprise he had planned for her birthday on Tuesday would change her heart and she wouldn't turn him down a third time.

Rejoicing that her spirits had lifted from when he'd first spotted her out on that jetty two hours earlier, Heath headed home to get ready. He had just enough time to do so before the evening service.

Sporting a clean pair of jeans and a long-sleeved cotton shirt, he shrugged into his jacket. More than good enough for the steakhouse on main where he was meeting Hudson after church. On the verge of running late, he dashed out of the camper to his trusty truck.

The service was great, the worship amazing. Heath missed one thing in the service though—seeing Reese seated in the pews.

After greeting the congregation at the end of the service, Heath left as soon as he could. At the restaurant, he found his brother already waiting at their table. Hudson shot to his feet. He glanced at his wristwatch. "Seven-thirty. Perfect timing. You hungry?"

Heath grinned. "Starved."

Hudson returned the grin. "Good. Because I happen to know that there's a steak in that kitchen with your name on it. My treat."

With a clap to Hudson's shoulder before he sat down, Heath joked, "Are you sure you can afford it, now that you're just a small town doctor?"

"I think I'll manage." Hudson chuckled. "I can always come to my brother for a loan if I get into trouble. Not so?"

A young waitress appeared at their table, burgundy leather menus in hand. She set them down on the table in front of each of them and smiled. "There you go, gents. I'll give you a few minutes to decide. In the meantime, can I take your drink order?"

After ordering two pops and a large sparkling water, they opened the menus and began scrutinizing the contents. Heath quickly settled on the Black Angus ribeye topped with blue cheese. Hudson, on the other hand, took his sweet time in making a selection.

"So, how did the house-hunting go today?" Heath asked as he shut the menu and set it aside.

Hudson glanced up. "Not great. I think I might have to fire this real estate agent and find another. She showed me everything I did not ask for in a house. Totally not the kinds of places I could see myself living in—way too fancy, way too big. I think she thought 'doctor, loads of money, big commission.' I'm not looking for a house; I'm looking for a home."

Heath's lips pursed, feeling his brother's frustration. Why didn't people listen? "I wish I could be of more help, but I've never had a need to look at the property market in Chapel Cove, so I can't say I know any real estate agents. But, I'll ask around."

"Thanks. I'm still confident my house is out there, and that I'll find it soon enough. Plus, I do have your generous offer to take up if this takes longer than I anticipate. Which is very likely, it seems. It's not as if Chapel Cove has a glut of houses for sale." Hudson lowered his gaze to the menu again.

Skewing his mouth, Heath bit down on the corner of his lip.

"Yeah...about that. I sort of offered the house to Reese earlier."

Hudson's head shot up from where he'd buried it in the menu. "You did what? Either you did offer it to Reese or you didn't. So which is it?"

"I did. I'm really sorry, I know I'd said you could stay there earlier this week, but she's in a dire situation. And I'm in a position to help."

Eyes narrowing, Hudson said, "It's all right. Just don't get taken for a ride, that's all. I don't want to see you get hurt again. And especially not by Reese."

"I won't. Anyway, it's not a given that she'll accept my offer. She's thinking about it."

The waitress returned with their drink order and set the two pops and bottled water down on the table.

Heath lifted his glass to his mouth, quenching his thirst. Hudson's reaction had left his mouth dry and his spirit troubled. Reese wouldn't use him, would she?

Did it matter?

"I have to help her, Hudson. I love her. Always have, always will. And I intend to win her back now that she's free."

Hudson's brows rose. "In that case, I hope she moves into your house, and that she stays...as Mrs. Brock. It's past time you put a ring on that girl's finger and married her."

He couldn't agree more.

Humph, if she'd let him.

Wait, negativity would get him nowhere. He would remain positive about this second chance. He wouldn't cease in his prayers nor let his hope wane.

Heath's lips parted in a grin. "Now that would be something, wouldn't it?"

CHAPTER THIRTEEN

REESE THREW back the bedcovers and tried to muster the energy to get up and face the day. She slithered from the bed, and with sloth-like movements, dragged herself down the passage toward the bathroom.

How did she get to this place in life? Forty and nowhere to go but downhill—although her life had already been sliding in that direction for the past few months.

Not even the dinner date Nai had planned for tonight at the fancy seafood restaurant on the boardwalk could summon up any excitement about her birthday. Nai had insisted she was treating Reese and Kristina, considering their situations. Seemed Nai had come to realize the importance of commemorating their fortieth birthdays—even though celebrating was the last thing Reese felt like doing at the moment.

And tomorrow, there'd be more celebrating for Kristina's birthday with coffee and cake in the afternoon at Ivy's on Spruce.

Reese had a sneaking suspicion that Nai now understood how crucial it was to give Dr. Johnson time with Aunt Ivy. Of course, the doctor had no qualms about watching over the woman he loved—even if this would be the third day in a row…well almost. He didn't have to stay with Aunt Ivy at all yesterday.

Reese huffed out a sigh. If only there was something that could brighten her mood.

Or someone…

She'd really thought Heath might've remembered it was her birthday—an important one—and asked her out for dinner. However, she *had* turned him down recently for breakfast and then again last night for dinner. Did she really expect him to be willing to face yet another rejection? Especially so soon?

Except, maybe this time she wouldn't say no. Even if it meant having to cancel with her friends. They'd understand, wouldn't they?

After brushing her teeth, Reese dragged herself downstairs to the kitchen, still clad in her pajamas. As she pushed open the half-closed door, her mom and dad began to sing happy birthday to her.

Dad wrapped his arms around Reese. Eyes brimming, he planted a soppy kiss on her cheek. "Happy birthday, sweetheart. May our good Lord bless you abundantly this year."

Reese swallowed the lump that formed in her throat. "Thanks, Dad." And somehow she had a feeling that God had already begun to show her favor, not that she deserved it at all. She'd wandered from her childhood promises to follow him, just as Lloyd had strayed from the vows he'd made to her at the altar.

Her heart ached, realizing how Jesus must've felt all these years she'd played the lost sheep. An image filled her mind—a throwback from her Sunday School days—of a smiling Savior walking on a mountain edge, a tiny black lamb wrapped around his shoulders. That was her! Jesus didn't react to betrayal in the way humans did. Instead of running in the other direction, not wanting anything to do with those who've lost their way, lost their first love, He went in search of them, determined to find His lost children and bring them home.

The lump in her throat returned with a vengeance, her eyes burned, and the pain in her heart deepened.

I'm so sorry, Lord. Forgive me?

Mom's hug pulled her back to the present.

"May it be a wonderful year for you, darling, filled with new beginnings and happiness. I pray that God will grant you the desires of your heart, Reese. Happy birthday."

The desires of her heart? Everything that had escaped her for over two decades—a husband who loved her deeply, one who wanted to father her children, and most of all, to once again live a life pleasing to the One who gave everything for her.

"Reese…" Mom held out an envelope. "We didn't know what to get you for your birthday, but figured you probably needed this most."

Taking the envelope, Reese lifted the flap and slid out a birthday card. As she opened the card, something fluttered to the floor. She bent over and picked up the rectangular piece of paper, her eyes widening in shock when she realized what it was.

"Mom, Dad, you can't— This is too much." Although the thousand-dollar check would go a long way to helping her back onto her feet. Add that to Heath's generous offer of the house, and suddenly life wasn't looking that gloomy. Maybe she would rise above her circumstances after all—with God's help.

Dad's hand enfolded hers. "Keep it, Reese. We know you need it. We've made some good investments over the past couple of years. We wouldn't be giving you this if we couldn't afford it."

"Thanks, Mom and Dad. You're the best!" Even as she said the words, and meant them, she couldn't help feeling a little slighted. If her parents could afford to give her so much money, why couldn't she just stay with them?

As if reading her mind, her father continued, "And in case you're wondering why we've given you the money, why you couldn't remain at home, it's because we love you. If we allowed you to stay, and you might never find your feet again. The strong, independent woman that you've always been, that we've always loved and admired, might be lost forever. We don't want to risk that happening."

Understanding sank in as to the motivation behind her parents' seemingly cruel decision, and Reese determined that she *would* make them proud of her once more. She needed to grow up in more ways than one.

Swiping at the tears moistening her cheeks, Mom asked, "You ready for breakfast?"

Reese smiled, her spirits lifting fast. "Always, Mom. You know that. But before we eat, I have some good news for you." They'd be happy to hear about Heath's kind offer. And Mom would certainly be eagerly reading between the lines to see if there was a chance for romance there too. Reese hoped her mother got her wish.

"Can it wait a few minutes?" Mom grabbed Reese's hand. "There's something else we need to show you first."

Dad followed behind them as Mom dragged Reese into the living room. Reese's gaze instantly settled on the low coffee table that stood between the couches. Perched on the wooden surface was the biggest bunch of red roses, beautifully arranged in a glass vase.

"For me?" Hand to her chest, Reese rushed forward.

Mom's laughter filled the room. "We have no idea who they're from, but please, read the card quickly and put your poor father and me out of our misery."

Reese plucked the small card from between the blooms. Who *were* they from? Couldn't be Lloyd, surely. And hopefully not Roman. She took the card out of its envelope and opened it, her pulse racing as she read.

Forty roses for the most beautiful forty-year-old I've ever known. Happy birthday, Reese. All my love, Heath.

P.S. Third time lucky? Have dinner with me tonight?

At the very bottom of the card, his cell number had been strategically placed.

After a breakfast with her parents where her Mom couldn't stop grinning, Reese headed upstairs to her room. She needed to text her friends.

She made her bed then plopped down on it and began typing on her phone.

WOULD YOU HATE ME VERY MUCH IF I CANCELED OUR PLANS FOR TONIGHT?

She sent a group text to both Nai and Kristina. Then, holding onto her phone, she leaned back against the headboard and waited for them to respond. Nai was the first to answer.

WOULD YOU HATE ME VERY MUCH IF I SAID CANCELING WOULD BE A BLESSING?! ;) AUNT IVY HAD A DIFFICULT NIGHT. ALL I WANT TO DO TONIGHT IS CRAWL INTO BED EARLY. BUT WHAT'S THE REASON YOU NEED TO CANCEL? OH, BY THE WAY, HAPPY BIRTHDAY AND WELCOME TO THE FORTIES CLUB.

Reese waited a while for Kristina to respond. After a few minutes, she did.

HMM, HAS THIS CHANGE OF PLAN GOT ANYTHING TO DO WITH A

CERTAIN HANDSOME YOUTH PASTOR? IS HE PLANNING TO TAKE YOU
OUT SOMEWHERE SPECIAL?

Reese typed back.

LOL, KRIS. AND NAI, THANKS FOR THE WELCOME, I THINK. HEATH
SENT ME FORTY ROSES THIS MORNING AND AN INVITATION TO
DINNER. I SHOULD PROBABLY ACCEPT. I'VE ALREADY TURNED HIM
DOWN TWICE—HE'S HOPING FOR THIRD TIME LUCKY. DON'T WANT
TO DISAPPOINT THE MAN.

Not long after Reese had sent the message, her phone buzzed.
Nai once again.

SQUEEE! LUCKY GIRL. AND GIVE THE GUY A BREAK, PLEEESE.
HE'S ONLY BEEN WAITING A LIFETIME FOR YOU.

Another buzz. Kristina. Her friend responded with one word.

YAY!

Relief flooded over Reese followed by the same excitement
she'd felt when they'd turned thirteen. Did her friends' approval of
this date mean they'd given their blessing to this relationship? Not
that it was a relationship.

Yet.

She had one more person to contact, but this she wouldn't do
via text. A phone call was so much more personal.

She dialed Heath's number, her heart beating faster with each
ring.

After basting the salmon with lemon and herbs, Heath covered the
dish with foil. He'd pop that into the oven just before he left to
fetch Reese.

Leaning against the counter, Heath surveyed his handiwork.
Everything was ready. All he had to do once they returned was
flash fry the baby carrots and green beans and add their respective

flavorings.

The dining room table had been set with the finest china, cutlery, crystal, and linen Uncle Trafford had owned. Only the long, white candles still needed to be lit.

And the living room... Perfect for a romantic birthday party for two. Candles standing ready, a fire ready to be lit in the antique fireplace, enough logs stacked beside it to last a few hours, and rose petals scattered on the floor.

He smiled.

Everything was perfect.

Heath had switched his day off yesterday with today. And just as well—he would've been of little use to the Lord had he been at work. Since Reese's phone call that morning, Heath had been able to concentrate on little other than his plans with her tonight. Between the grocery store, the florist, and his house to make tonight special, he'd done a lot of running.

His house?

Well, that was a first. He'd always referred to this place as Uncle Trafford's place. Now he could actually see himself living here one day with Reese at his side.

Heath turned to gaze out of the window at the marina and the ocean. His camper had an awesome view, but the sight before his eyes was pretty incredible too. He hadn't paid attention to its wuthering heights in so long, only coming and going from the house these past few years to let summer renters in and out, do laundry and fetch clothes once a week, and to use his dark room.

Noticing the time on the kitchen clock, he sprang into action. Only thirty minutes to shower and dress, pop the salmon in the oven, and hustle on over to Reese's door.

He could do it.

Bounding up the stairs, taking them two at a time, he rushed to the second floor.

Minutes later, towel wrapped around his waist, hair damp from the quick shower, Heath stared into the spare room's closet. He kept most of his clothing there, simply because the camper didn't have much space. He'd swap outfits when necessary when he came to the house to do his laundry.

With no time to spare, Heath opted for something between smart and casual. Couldn't go wrong with that look tonight. He donned the pair of dark jeans and white, collared shirt, pulling on a black sweater over that to keep out the cold on his travels between his house and Reese's. He decided on his trusty Chelsea boots— easy enough to slip out of when he wanted to get comfortable, but not over-the-top.

Downstairs, he slid the baking dish with the salmon into the oven. As soon as he got home, he'd light up that fire he'd prepared.

After checking, again, that the small box was safely tucked in his jacket pocket, he headed for the garage. Tonight called for a fancier ride than his old truck. Uncle Trafford's luxury sedan, now also Heath's property, would provide that.

He planned to offer Reese the car as well for her use, but not just yet. He didn't want to smother her with kindness lest she think he was trying to ensure she was indebted to him. He had to be certain she realized that whatever kindnesses he offered came with no strings attached—that everything he did came from the purest motivation because he loved her.

Soon, the silver Tesla pulled up outside the Aylward residence. Heath made his way up the path then knocked on the front door, his heart pounding harder than his knuckles.

The door opened. Reese's father stood on the other side, smiling. "Evening, Pastor Heath." He held out his hand, and Heath shook it.

"Evening, Mr. Aylward. And please, it's just Heath."

The elderly man nodded. "All right, Heath. Please, come inside.

Reese will be down in a minute. I hope." His soft chuckle filled the entrance hall as he closed the door. "She's changed outfits a number of times."

Heath's heart thumped in his chest at the thought that she found it important to look good tonight.

"Hello, Pastor Heath."

The sound of Reese's mother's voice drew his attention to the staircase. He lifted his gaze.

She waved from the second floor landing. "Reese will be downstairs in just a moment. Maybe."

"Hi, Mrs. Aylward. I'm glad to hear that." He wanted to add "because the salmon will spoil if she takes too long", but he didn't want Reese to get any inkling that *he* was cooking for her tonight. "Oh, and it's just Heath, by the way. Let's reserve the title for Pastor Don."

A door clicked upstairs and Heath's pulse thrummed. Any minute now, the birthday girl would appear.

And she did, looking every inch the Vogue cover model she'd always been. Nobody could ever take that away from her.

Reese navigated the staircase like a pro. She'd chosen an elegant, ivory-colored halterneck blouse, and in her hand, she carried a black jacket. Her high-waist slacks and heeled boots, both matching her jacket, made her legs appear even longer.

She'd swept her hair up and pinned it, leaving her creamy shoulders on display. He could already feel the softness of her skin beneath his fingers.

Hmm, maybe dinner at his house wasn't a good idea after all. It would've been far safer to take her out to a restaurant. But hadn't he done that once before and look how that had turned out. That option held no guarantees that they wouldn't still end up doing something they'd regret.

Please, Lord, protect us from making any mistakes tonight.

Lead us not into temptation.

Mrs. Aylward followed behind Reese, beaming from ear to ear. It was good to see that her mother seemed to approve of this date.

As Reese took the last step, Heath moved forward. "You look incredible."

Tipping her head, she smiled. "You look pretty handsome yourself."

His heart thudded at her words.

Gently clasping her upper arms, Heath leaned forward and kissed her cheek. "Happy birthday, Reese." How he would've loved to rather press his lips to hers, but he didn't want to disrespect her parents.

The same soft floral notes that he remembered from their time at the hospital in Portland drew him back to the kisses they'd shared that night in the truck. Even though reluctant to push away the memory of that encounter, Heath released her and asked, "Shall we go?"

Reese nodded, and Heath helped her into her jacket.

"Bye, Mom and Dad. You'll probably be asleep by the time I get home, so I'll see you tomorrow." Reese kissed her parents then turned to Heath, her mouth curving. "Oh, thank you for the roses. They're absolutely beautiful; I have them in my room. You made me feel really special."

Heath smiled. "Absolutely my pleasure."

As they stepped into the fresh night air, he glanced back at Reese's parents. "I promise not to have her home too late."

Mrs. Aylward waved his promise away. "There's no need for a curfew, Heath—Reese is a grown woman, and we know that we can trust you. It's a special birthday. Just go and enjoy yourselves without watching the clock."

Yes, they could trust him now. But sadly, there was a time when that wasn't true.

It wasn't only the cold air that took Reese's breath away as she stepped outside. She stared at the sleek silver ride parked outside her parents' house as they strolled down the garden path toward the street. Heath certainly was pulling out all the stops today.

"Wow, fancy wheels. Whose are they?" she asked, breathing a sigh of relief that she didn't have to travel in the pick-up tonight.

"Uncle Trafford's."

Reese paused for a moment to look up at him. "So you mean, yours? Or did your uncle bequeath that car to one of your other brothers and you're just keeping it safe?"

A low rumble bubbled from Heath's chest. "Yes, I mean it's mine, although I haven't gotten used to that fact because I barely drive it."

No way. Surely not? She had to clarify she'd heard right.

"You've barely driven this beautiful car in five years? That's how long your uncle has been gone, right?"

"Thereabouts." Heath opened the door for Reese.

Before getting inside the luxury vehicle, Reese raised a brow at Heath. "You really should get out more." With a smile, she slid onto the leather seat, keeping her gaze fixed on him.

Heath chuckled. "You're so right. But I intend to change that, starting tonight." He winked and shut the door before rounding the car to the driver's side.

Once they'd buckled up, Heath started the engine. Soft classical sounds drifted from the radio.

Closing her eyes, Reese inhaled deeply of the spicy cologne Heath wore tonight, and her head swirled. The music wasn't the only pleasantly distracting thing to fill the cabin.

Clothes, car, cologne… Heath Brock was definitely pulling out all the stops tonight, and she couldn't wait to see what he had lined up for dinner.

Mesmerized, Heath watched as Reese dabbed her mouth with the napkin then folded it. She set the cloth down next to her empty dessert plate and pushed the dish away. Wearing a more-than-satisfied smile, she relaxed back into her seat. The candlelight reflected in her eyes, making them dance.

"You cooked all that, for me? I'm impressed."

Heath held up his hands in surrender. "Full disclosure, I cheated on the triple chocolate mousse cake. Aileen's Pastries gets the credit for all that decadence."

"Well, kudos to you for realizing where to draw the line on your kitchen skills, *and* for knowing the best place to rectify that."

Heath leaned forward, pasting his most serious look on his face for a moment. "I can bake." He burst out laughing. "But nowhere near as well as Aileen."

"Nobody can bake like Aileen, or so I hear." The faint upward quirk of her mouth tattled on her smothered laugh.

"You heard right." Heath shoved his chair back and rose. "Should we move to the living room? We can enjoy coffee beside the fire."

The central heating in the house had ensured no chilly rooms tonight, but the crackling fire would hopefully guarantee no chilly hearts. At least, Reese's. His heart, well the flames of love burned brighter than they ever had.

"That would be nice." Reese started to stand, and Heath rushed over to ease the chair out of her way. She glanced over her shoulder at him. "Thank you. Do you need help with the coffee? The dishes?"

Heath shook his head and steered her toward the living room.

"Rose petals? Candles? Very romantic, Heath."

All for you, Reese. All for you.

"You get comfortable on that couch while I pour the coffee." Heath stooped to throw fresh logs onto the glowing coals before leaving.

By the time he returned, two large mugs in his hands, the logs had taken flame. Reese had let her hair down, kicked off her boots, and tucked her feet beneath her. She hugged one of the scatter cushions to her chest.

Oh, honey, you could hug me instead.

Heath set the mugs down on the low table then sat down beside her. "We'll need to let that cool for a few minutes. I used hot milk. A little too hot."

"That's all right. I need that chocolate mousse cake to settle a while longer anyway." Eyes shining, she smiled at him. "So, what are we going to do while we wait for the coffee to cool?"

Mercy. Heath steeled himself, determined to phrase a safe response. "If it was still light, we could've gazed across the ocean and enjoyed the view. And if it was already summer, we could've opened the doors, enjoyed the breeze, and listened to the ocean."

"But it's neither light nor summer." Reese pouted her full, peach-colored lips. "So what *are* we to do after such a perfect evening?"

Oh blast. Forget the safe response. He wanted her in his arms as much as it seemed she wanted to be there. One kiss. Just one.

Heath inched closer and trailed his fingers slowly up her arm. Her skin was softer than he remembered. "We *could* end this perfect evening in the most perfect way." His gaze drifted to her lips.

With a giggle, Reese clamped the corner of her mouth. "And that is…?"

"This." He drew her into his arms. Finger to her chin, he tipped her head. Their lips met with a hunger that Heath knew could never really be satisfied. He'd always want to feast on her kisses until he was old and gray.

Finally, Reese broke the kiss and relaxed back into the couch, long reddish-blond strands spilling over the fabric. "That was the best birthday gift you could ever have given me. And it was way sweeter and far more decadent than any dessert Aileen could ever make."

Gift...Oh brother, he'd almost forgotten the most important part of the night.

"Wait right here!" Heath sprang to his feet and sprinted to the front door where their jackets hung on the coat stand. He retrieved the small, gift box from his jacket pocket then made his way back to Reese.

He sank onto the cushions and handed her the gift. "I almost forgot. No birthday is complete without a birthday gift."

Reese stared at the small box in her hand. "Oh, Heath…"

"Go on. Open it. I hope it's to your taste."

Hands trembling, she slid the white, satin ribbon from the black box then lifted the lid. Hand to her mouth, she gasped. "It's beautiful. But, Heath, it's too much. You can't give me something like this."

Heath pressed a finger to her lips. "Shh." He removed the diamond pendant from its velvety bed. "This is only the first to replace all that you lost. Turn around and let me help you put it on."

Reese shifted on the couch, offering Heath her back. She lifted her hair, and Heath fastened the necklace around her neck.

Twisting around again, she gazed down at the solitaire diamond sparkling at the end of the white gold chain. She touched the stone and whispered, "It's beautiful."

Reese planted a quick kiss on Heath's mouth. "Thank you. You have made this birthday that I so dreaded very special."

"I'm glad." Heath swallowed hard. He would love to return that kiss, and then some, but he didn't want to spoil their fresh start. And too many kisses from this woman could turn to other things.

Leaning forward, Heath grabbed the two mugs. He handed one to Reese. "I should probably get you home soon; I promised your parents I'd return you at a reasonable hour. So, drink up."

Reese pressed her free palm to his chest. "And did you forget that my mom said we were to take our time and enjoy ourselves?"

"No, I haven't, but if we don't go soon, I might want to hold on to you all night. And I don't want to mess up anything with you. Not again." He cupped her cheek, his thumb smoothing her skin. "I love you, Reese. I've never stopped loving you. And I want to do things right this time, if you'll let me."

Chapter Fourteen

REESE IGNORED the ringing of her phone for as long as possible. She wanted to stay in dreamland with Heath. Finally accepting that the insistent caller wasn't going away, she groaned and reached for the offensive device she'd left on the night stand. She wiped her eyes and tried to focus on the screen.

Unknown number. Should she answer, or just ignore it?

But if she ignored the call, it would bother her all day long wondering who'd tried to contact her.

Lying on her side, she swiped the green phone icon on the screen. She'd be highly annoyed if it was some salesperson trying to sell her something. Too late now. If it was, she'd decline as politely as it was in her DNA to do and cut the call.

She shoved the phone between the pillow and her ear, and mumbled, "Reese Aylward."

"Reese, it's Roman. I'm sorry to contact you this early."

Reese glanced at the time on her bedside clock. Eight a.m. Not *that* early, but long before she'd intending on rising. She'd only returned home last night around midnight. After promising Heath she'd keep her distance on one side of the couch if he was able to stay on the other side, she'd managed to convince him to let her stay a while longer. It was her birthday, after all, she'd protested. He hadn't been able to refuse.

Once he'd sweetly kissed her goodnight at her parents' front door, she'd gone straight upstairs to bed. But sleep hadn't come easy as, over and over, she relived Heath's kisses and his declaration of love. She'd so wanted to tell him that she loved him too, probably always had, but she had to be absolutely sure.

Hah, as if she wasn't already!

At least she'd agreed they could see where this led.

Did that mean they were officially dating?

Guess so.

"Reese? Are you still there?"

"Y–yes, I'm here. Is something wrong?" Why else would he be calling her? Oh, she hoped it wasn't to ask her out. She really should never have flirted with him at church on Sunday.

"Didn't you get the text from Kristina? I assumed since Nai got one, as did I, you would've too."

Text?

"I'm sorry, no. I was out last night and didn't have my phone with me." She'd deliberately left it at home and hadn't looked at it until it woke her moments ago.

"What was the text about? Your sister wants vanilla cake now instead of chocolate?" A chuckle bubbled from her mouth. "Oh, by the way, happy birthday to you. Glad you'll also be celebrating later with us girls."

"She canceled her birthday," Roman blurted.

"What?" Reese shoved herself upright and leaned against the headboard, suddenly more awake. She raked her hair away from her face, tucking it behind her ears. "Nobody can cancel a birthday. It happens...every year, same date, whether we like it or not."

Roman's sigh drifted through the phone. "Well, my sister did."

"Why?" It was bad enough that Reese had had to cancel on her friends the previous night. Now Kristina too?

"Um, let's just say she's really upset and leave it at that. I want to help her, but I think I need reinforcements. You and Nai have been friends with her forever. Could you meet me at her house in say an hour? And bring cake. Lots of it. Chocolate."

An hour? Didn't give her much time to shower and get dressed. She didn't want to go out not looking her best. Chapel Cove was small, and she could bump into Heath anywhere, anytime. She needed to look good for her man.

Her man? Oh, she did like the sound of that.

Then she would need to call Nai to come get her. Once ready, she'd have to wolf down breakfast while waiting for her friend. She got really cranky if she didn't have the most important meal of the day. And then, before going to Kristina's house, they'd need to make a stop at Aileen's to get cake.

Way, way too much to do in a short hour. And that didn't even take into account their driving time.

"How about ten a.m.? Will that work for you?" Reese asked.

"Perfect. See you soon. And Reese, thanks. Will you let Nai know? She said she'd be fine with whatever worked for you."

"No problem. My friends would do the same for me."

Reese cut the call and sprang out of bed like a bullfrog at a fly. Fortunately, in twenty-two years, she'd learned the art of the quick change.

At ten on the dot, Nai pulled outside Kristina's stone-colored, one-story rental. As they walked to the front door, each bearing a box of treats, Reese couldn't help wondering who'd trimmed Kristina's lawn so well.

Probably Kristina. She was such a hands-on woman. Practical. So unlike Reese.

The door swung open and Kristina stood on the other side. She looked awful, with a capital A. As much as Reese couldn't wait to spill the beans and tell her two friends that she was back with Heath, in a manner of speaking, now was definitely not the right time. Good thing she'd tucked that gorgeous diamond pendant into her blouse to hide it from Nai until she could tell them both.

With Roman's help, they quickly went to work plying Kristina with coffee and cake around her dining room table. Eventually, Kristina unloaded the news about her rotten ex's ultimatum to go back to him that had brought her life to a screeching halt. Thankfully, jokes slowly started to fly between the twin siblings, and Reese was reminded of a birthday party so long ago, sans Roman, where they'd all ended up wearing cake in the same manner that Kristina had just threatened to do to her brother.

Reese wasn't the only one thinking about the same birthday party, because Kristina suddenly reminded them that today was the day they'd planned to dig up the treasures and lists they'd buried twenty-seven years ago.

Reese had completely forgotten about that pact, until now.

As she recalled the five things she'd written down, sadness filled her. Some things she'd achieved—though not necessarily in the right way. Others she'd neglected. And on one item she had totally missed the mark, and it might be too late to achieve it.

Yes, she'd become a supermodel, and way quicker than she'd thought too. But what had it been worth? She'd walked away with nothing, her fame soon lost. All she had left were the memories. Good and bad.

Yes, she'd kissed Heath Brock. More than that, she'd lost her virginity to him. And she hadn't stuck around long enough for him to make an honest woman out of her as he'd wanted.

Yes, she'd lived a life sold out for Jesus…until she was almost eighteen. Then she'd gotten caught up in the world of fashion and Lloyd, and Jesus was soon forgotten. Although, her husband and career couldn't be solely blamed. Her guilt over what had happened with Heath had been the catalyst for her spiritual decline.

She didn't have a husband who loved and adored her. In fact, had Lloyd ever really loved her? Certainly not in the way Heath did.

And she didn't have a single child, let alone the two or three she'd always wanted.

Maybe being back in Chapel Cove, she'd be able to rectify those last three things. Already she'd made things right with God and was in the process of putting that relationship back on track. And after last night, she certainly had hope for a future with Heath too.

Kneeling beside the shallow hole where they'd buried that beautiful biscuit tin so long ago, Reese lifted the treasure chest and set it down on the small pile of unearthed soil. It didn't look so beautiful now, the images she'd loved long gone and tinged now with rust.

She glanced at her friends. "Wasn't this burial site much farther away from the large spruce?" Many trees hugged the surrounding cliffs; this was the only one of its kind growing so close to the south side of the tiny chapel that overlooked the cove.

Nai shook her head and smiled. "Everything seemed larger than life at thirteen. Remember, we've grown from little girls into women."

That was so true. And as women, they no longer looked at the world through rose-colored glasses.

Reese lifted the lid on the tin and reached inside to retrieve the Ziploc bag with her treasures. Good move on her part to have thought to protect their items in the small, plastic, self-seal bags.

She clutched the bag to her chest for a moment. Nai and Kristina were equally quiet, the moment solemn for them all.

Opening her bag, Reese turned it upside down, and the shell bracelet she'd made for Heath one long ago afternoon slid onto her palm. She folded her fingers around the shells. So many years and she'd come full circle.

In an instant, Reese knew what she wanted to do with the rest of her life.

She shoved to her feet.

Nai and Kristina's head's shot up, their eyes questioning.

"I–I need to make a phone call," Reese blurted out before hurrying away.

Leaning against the white, aged walls of the stone chapel, Reese dialed Heath's number.

He answered on the third ring. "This is a pleasant surprise. Missing me already?"

Reese smiled. Oh, she was so going to enjoy having him back in her life. Teasing and all. "I am. Listen, do you think you can come get me? Now. I'm up at the chapel on the cove."

"Sure. It's lunch time anyway. I'll be there in a few minutes."

"Thanks."

In the time she waited for Heath's red pickup to drive down the narrow lane to the chapel, Reese explained her future plans to her friends.

The truck pulled to a stop close by, and Heath clambered out.

Nai jabbed her elbow into Reese's side. "He's way taller than I remembered. And far more good looking." She grinned. "You go, girl."

Heath waved as he strode toward them. "Morning, ladies." Without hesitating, he drew Reese into a hug and kissed her—right there in front of her childhood friends. Good thing she'd just told them what he'd said last night. And about his offer of the house. Nai and Kristina were extremely relieved when she explained that it wasn't the camper on the beach.

Clicking his fingers, Heath pointed at Kristina. "It's your birthday today, right?" He turned to Nai. "And wasn't it yours a few days ago?"

Kristina and Nai nodded.

"Well, happy birthday." He gave them each a brief hug then turned to Reese. "You ready?"

Ready as she'd ever be.

As they drove away, Heath turned to Reese. "What was so urgent? Not that I'm complaining about getting to see you today."

"This." She withdrew the bracelet from her jacket pocket and laid it on his thigh. "I made it for you just before I turned thirteen. But then I got cold feet and ended up burying it along with a wish list Nai, Kristina, and I each made. I–I wanted you to have it, even though it's doubtful it'll still fit."

Heath glanced down at his leg then lifted the bracelet, sliding it around his fingers. He brushed the shells with his thumb as he examined it. "You made this for *me*?"

She nodded.

"I love it. But you're right—there's no way it'll fit my wrist now. However, I know just the place for it." He attached the bracelet to his rearview mirror. "Now I can see it all the time."

Reese sucked in a deep breath to still the nervous fluttering in her stomach.

Heath shot her a look. "What is it?"

"D–do you think I can move into your house today? Seeing that bracelet again made me remember something that made me really happy. Something I could see myself doing for the rest of my days."

"Being my wife? Bearing my children?" Heath's eyes lit with his grin.

"Besides that." Although the thought of being Mrs. Heath Brock and having a few little Brocks running around the house *was* most appealing. "I want to start my own jewelry line made from local coastal materials—seashells, agates, sea glass…so many possibilities. I figure it'll take a few months' work to stock up, so I'd like to get started right away. Your house will afford me the space I need to work. Maybe by the summer I'll be able to open up a small shop on the boardwalk."

"If I weren't driving, Reese Aylward, I'd give you the biggest hug ever. That's a fantastic idea. And you know I'll be right there beside you, supporting you, helping you, cheering you on."

She nodded. "I know."

Heath reached over and trailed his fingers lightly through her hair. Then he blew her a kiss. "Why don't I take you to the house to get the car so that you can start moving in? Unfortunately, I have a counseling session at two that I can't cancel, but I'll get back as soon as I can."

"Sounds great. Thanks, Heath." Reese shifted closer to him and planted a kiss on his cheek. Taking his hand in hers, she promised herself to never let him go.

Not this time.

Alone inside Bliant's Bluff, Reese made herself a cup of coffee then stepped out onto the porch to drink in the view. A chilly breeze wafted toward her from the sea as she sipped her hot drink.

Her insides warmed.

She gazed across the ocean, thinking about her move. It wouldn't take long. After all, she only possessed one suitcase of clothing, and her bicycle would have to wait until Heath was back so that it could be loaded onto his truck.

The longest part of moving would be telling her mom and dad about her plans. They'd be certain to have a lot of questions.

Her phone rang, invading her thoughts. Another unknown number. All had turned out well when she answered Roman's call earlier. She slid her finger across the phone and brought the device to her ear. "Hello, this is Reese speaking."

"Clarise, my darling."

Reese gasped. "Aunt Ivy! What are you doing making phone calls? Shouldn't you be resting?"

"Oh, phooey. I'm not that incapacitated that I can't give you a call to wish you birthday blessings. I did try last night, several times in fact, but got no answer."

Paying little attention to her phone over the past twenty-four hours, Reese hadn't even noticed she had missed calls.

"I'm sorry, Aunt Ivy. I was out and my phone was at home."

"Oooh." Aunt Ivy sang the word more than she spoke it. "A birthday date? I hope it was someone worthy of spending such a momentous occasion with you. It's not every day a girl turns forty. And now the fun really begins because you're older and you're wiser. With all you girls finally back together in Chapel Cove, maybe you'll get a do-over. From what I've heard and seen, life hasn't exactly turned out the way you'd all planned."

If only Aunt Ivy knew how much truth lay in her words of wisdom.

"I spent it with Heath Brock. A good choice, I think." Reese giggled, feeling much like a schoolgirl once again today.

"Heathcliff? A fabulous choice indeed, Clarise. He's a

wonderful man. You'll do well not to let that one go, my dear. Good stock, the Brock men. Good stock."

"Heathcliff?" Did Aunt Ivy mean her Heath?

Aunt Ivy's soft laugh floated through the phone. "I know everyone calls him Heath, or Pastor Brock, but thanks to his Uncle Trafford who always called the boy by his full name, I got into the habit too. Please, send him my best regards when next you see him. And tell him that I'm receiving visitors now and look forward to him stopping by."

"I will, Aunt Ivy. Thanks so much for calling."

Reese shoved the phone back into her jacket pocket and hurried inside.

Deep in thought, she paced the living room floor, her eyes constantly drawn to those six photographs.

Wuthering Heights. Heathcliff. Surely it couldn't be?

But it would explain so much if it was. Like how Uncle Trafford, trailer and RV park owner, came to have six such expensive artworks hanging on his walls.

It would explain the abundance of Oregon sights in *Wuthering Heights'* photographs.

She had to know. And she had an idea where she could find the answer.

Boot heels tapped across the wooden floor as Reese hurried to the door off the scullery. Beyond there lay Heath's "hobby room".

Hobbies? She'd never known him to have any. Except photography. And he was pretty good at it. After all, it was his photos that had landed her a placement with Lloyd Barker's agency in New York.

Her fingers wrapped around the doorknob, and she tried turning it. Locked, drat.

Her eyes flitted around the scullery. No keys hanging anywhere, but beside the washing machine stood a narrow chest of drawers.

Maybe the key was in one of them.

Reese opened the top drawer and looked inside.

Dishtowels. Loads of them.

She stuck her hand inside, feeling toward the back of the drawer and under the cloths. Her fingers brushed against something. Instantly recognizing the key shape, she drew it into her palm.

Yes!

Hopefully she wasn't making the biggest mistake of her life by opening this door. Hadn't Heath kept it locked for a reason?

She cracked the door open and turned on the light to see a small room filled with photo developing equipment. This wasn't Heath's hobby room—this was his dark room. Photographs hung overhead, the familiar style of the artist easily recognizable. The world may not know who *Wuthering Heights* was, but she did.

Why hadn't Heath told her?

Much as he should've been disappointed when his two o'clock was a no show, Heath just couldn't be. Not today.

He rushed from his office at the church and out into the parking lot. He hopped into his pickup. Now he could help Reese move and settle her in. Maybe make dinner for her later.

Several minutes after leaving the school, Heath pulled the truck to a stop outside Uncle Trafford's house.

Um, correction, *his* house. This would take some getting used to, but it was time. Finally he had a reason to think of the place as his and to admit that he'd finally outgrown the need for the camper. Of course, he'd have to stay there a while longer, but when the time came, hopefully she'd say yes. He was putting his heart on the line and risking everything for this second shot with Reese. He couldn't make the same mistake of taking things *too* slowly again.

And he was almost certain that her feelings for him were strong. Maybe even strong enough to be defined as love.

He could only hope and pray.

Heath tried the front door. It opened at his touch. Great, it meant that Reese was still there as he'd hoped. Either that or she'd forgotten to lock the door on her way out.

He strode into the kitchen and called out, "Reese! Are you home?"

"In here," her voice filtered from the living room.

He rushed into the room to find Reese standing with her back to him, once again examining the photographs on the wall. He chuckled. "You really are fascinated with that artist, aren't you?"

She turned to him, arms folded. "Why didn't you tell me?"

Heath swallowed hard and slowly stepped closer. "Tell you what?"

"That you're him. *Wuthering Heights*... That's you. Those are your photographs, aren't they?"

"Hmm." Taking her hand, Heath led Reese to the couch. "Sit."

She sank onto the cushion.

He joined her. *Lord, please let her understand. Don't let me lose her over something like this. Not when we've just found each other again.*

His eyes searched hers. "Yes. Those are my photographs. I didn't want to tell you yet. I was waiting for the right moment."

"The right moment?" Confusion washed over her face.

"I–I needed a little time to tell if your feelings for me were genuine. I didn't want you to be with me because you felt I could provide for you in a similar manner to what you were accustomed. I needed to know whether you could be happy with the penniless youth pastor who still lived in the same camper of his youth."

Her gaze narrowed, and her eyes misted. "You think so little of me?"

"No... No! I think the world of you. But I needed to be sure what you could be satisfied with. We're only going to get one shot at this second chance, Reese. I want to get it right in every way." He reached for her hand.

She withdrew and inched away from him. "So you lied to me?"

"I've never lied to you, Reese."

"Really? You want to tell me that when I asked about how your uncle could afford those photographs, you didn't blatantly tell an untruth?"

He hadn't. He had sidestepped opening up to her, but he hadn't lied. Not blatantly, at least. Still, a lie of omission...

Forgive me, Lord.

"I should have told you. I'm sorry. Uncle Trafford wanted some photographs for the wall and asked if I'd shoot some for him. He insisted on paying me for the work. Of course, I didn't charge him what the galleries do. In fact, I didn't want to charge him at all. In the end, we came to a compromise and I gave him a *really* good family discount. Otherwise he might not have been able to afford the prints, even though his businesses had provided a good income for him. After all, he'd managed to buy this home and the car, but it had probably depleted his savings considerably. I think he'd done it to prepare for a future with Ivy. Then he got sick, and everything changed."

Heath blinked several times. It still choked him up to think of the suffering Uncle Trafford went through. He closed his eyes for a moment and breathed in deeply before continuing. "What I told you on Saturday was by no means a lie. Yes, I wasn't open with you—only because I felt it was too early to tell you everything. But I was honest. I've always been honest with you, Reese. Deep down, you know that."

She lowered her gaze, clearly pondering what he'd said.

Lord, help her to understand.

Heath waited patiently for a reaction, each passing second feeling like hours.

Her gazed fixed in front of her, Reese massaged her fingers. Finally, she opened her mouth. "Can I ask you one more thing?"

Heath covered her hands, quieting her self-pacifying. The situation seemed to cause her stress. "Anything."

"What made you decide to sell your works under a pseudonym? Why not sign your photographs Heath Brock?"

"I–it just felt right at the time. The name fit with the direction I was taking my photography, and thanks to Emily Brontë, it provided the connection to Heathcliff Brock. I guess my initial thinking was that if I ever did make it big, I didn't want the notoriety to interfere with being me—Heath Brock, youth pastor of whatever church I found myself serving at." Heath shrugged, unsure whether he'd explained himself well enough. "Does that make sense of why I found it necessary to separate the two aspects of my life?"

Reese nodded. "I think I understand."

Biting her bottom lip, she slowly looked up at him. "So does that mean you're extremely wealthy? Because you do know I'm well aware of what each of those photographs is worth."

He wanted to tease back, but this was the time for full disclosure, not jokes.

"I need to let you in on another secret—but only because I want you to know everything there is to know about Heathcliff Brock and *Wuthering Heights*, not because I have any desire to blow my own trumpet. When my photos became so sought after by society's elite, I made a conscious decision to tithe ninety percent of the earnings to the church, to certain charities, and to orphanages in Africa and Eastern Europe. You see, I don't take my photographs for the money but for the love of capturing that moment in time, immortalizing it forever."

Now he could grin. "So no, I'm not extremely wealthy, but I am pretty comfortable, because the more I give away, the more God blesses me."

"So you're not the penniless youth pastor everyone thinks you are? You're able to support a wife? Children?" Her eyes twinkled with mirth. Were her questions hinting at what he hoped?

Only one way to find out.

He slid a hand behind her head, cradling it while the other hand circled her waist. Gently easing her onto the couch, he kissed her, taking care to make it last just the right amount of time—not too long lest their passions sweep them away; not too short either. He would never want Reese to feel unsatisfied.

With a husky voice he whispered in her ear, hoping it was the answer she sought. "I have more than enough to support a wife and children. And I look forward to doing exactly that very soon."

CHAPTER FIFTEEN

Four weeks later…

THE WEATHERMAN forecast that the mercury would rise again today. Before it got too warm to comb the shores for shells, Reese hopped out of bed and peeked out of the window to make sure the forecast was correct.

Blue skies and an azure ocean greeted her, and in the marina, brightly colored hulls bobbed lazily on the water.

She released a satisfied sigh. She would never tire of this view. Only one thing was missing—having Heath share these beautiful mornings with her. But she had faith that any day now, he'd get down on one knee and once again ask her to marry him.

Quickly, Reese dressed in black jeans and matching sleeveless top, then slid her feet into a pair of open sandals, ones that were easy to kick off once she stepped onto the soft, sandy beach.

She donned her favorite black porkpie hat with white paisley band, slung a bag around her body for the shells, agates, and sea glass, and hopped onto her bike. She freewheeled all the way down the hill to the bridge crossing Sweetwater River.

She had found the perfect place to collect shells, not far from Heath's camper. Every morning, she would rise early and head down there on her bike. It was a great way to work out too, especially the uphill home. But she needed to keep herself in shape for Heath. Just because he'd waited twenty-two years for her, didn't mean he'd stick around if she let herself go. Although, somehow, deep down, she knew he would stay with her no matter what came their way.

Collecting the shells the ocean offered up every night, were like God's mercies—new every morning.

Some days, depending on his youth work schedule, Heath would join her, camera in hand. Together, they had brought a new dimension to his photographs, and every day as they strolled along the beaches or peered down from lofty cliffs, they prayed the art world would look favorably on the new inclusion to his work.

Heath sat waiting on the step of his camper as she pedaled toward him. He rose and before she could get off the bike, he gripped the handlebars. Leaning forward, his lips met hers. Oh what she wouldn't give to start every morning with a few of those kisses. Her pulse raced. Never had she been this happy.

"I've got news for you," he said, unable to contain his grin.

"I can barely wait to hear. But let me park my bike first then we can talk." Reese clambered off the bicycle and parked it against the usual black cottonwood. She kicked her sandals from her feet then tucked the shoes into the back pockets of her jeans.

Taking her hand, Heath led her onto the beach, the sound of seagulls drifting from where they skimmed the ocean in search of an early morning snack.

Reese had taken a few steps before she paused and dug her heels into the sand. "You're not taking your camera today? With such magnificent weather, you're bound to get the most amazing photos."

"Not today. I have other plans."

"Like helping me collect shells?" Reese glanced at Heath and continued on toward the line of shells left behind on the wet sand with the receding tide.

He shot her a mischievous smile. His right cheek dimpled, the depression darker against his stubbled chin. "Maybe. Maybe not."

Reese crinkled her nose at him. "You're acting weird today." Very weird. And what was with the jacket? It wasn't in the least bit cold. Probably wouldn't help to ask. She'd likely just get some vague answer.

"So, what's this news you have?" she asked.

Heath disappeared for a moment as he bent to scoop up some shells. He handed her a few. "These are good ones—they'll make stunning pendants."

"Thanks." Reese tipped her head and widened her eyes, not-so-patiently waiting for Heath to spill the news.

"Oh, yes. So, I had a call earlier from the gallery in New York—they can never seem to remember that I'm three hours behind them in time. Anyway, they love the new line of work with you subtly included in the images."

Reese's eyes widened. "Really? That's fantastic!" She jumped up and down, giggling as she twirled around. And here she'd thought her days in front of the camera were over forever. But Heath had made it happen all over again for her, in more meaningful and artistic ways. How she loved this man.

Heath nodded, placing his hands on Reese's shoulders to still her outburst. "They said to keep on sending them because this line was going to sell like hotcakes. And, they're pricing the series at twenty percent more than my previous images. That's how much faith they have in them."

"What? I can't believe it! No wait, I can. You're super-talented, as am I." Hand to her chest, she wiggled her hips. "And we both serve a mighty God who is able to do more than we could ever ask or imagine. All the glory belongs to Him."

"Amen." Heath grinned again, and Reese was convinced he had something up his sleeve. Maybe that's why he was wearing a jacket this morning.

"I told you God keeps on blessing me in abundance." He wrapped his arms around Reese's waist. Lifting her, he swung her around. "And you are the biggest blessing of all."

"Oh, Heath." She drew his head toward hers and her mouth brushed his.

Without hesitation, Heath deepened the kiss.

When their lips parted, Heath planted one knee in the sand. Taking Reese's hand in his, he gazed up at her. "Clarise Aylward, I love you with all my heart. I always have, and I always will. These past few weeks have been the happiest of my life. But all of a sudden, the camper feels small and lonely. Seems a shame not to share all that space in Uncle Trafford's home with someone else."

Reese giggled. "You mean *your* home."

"Of course, although I would rather have said '*our* home.' Please, honey, say you'll finally marry me and make me the happiest man alive." His hand disappeared into his jacket pocket. As he slid the ring onto her finger, the diamond glistened in the sunlight.

"Oh, Heath, you need to show Dr. Johnson how to make that move with Ivy."

Heath quirked an eyebrow and his head tipped to the side. "Babe, you're stalling. And don't worry about the doc, he'll get there, one day." Tiny lines formed at the corners of his eyes with his smile. "Now, for the last time, will you marry me, girl?"

"Yes! Yes, I'll marry you Heathcliff Brock." She fell to her knees in front of him and smoothed a hand through his hair, her eyes searching his. "Nothing will make me happier than to share my life with you, and *our* home."

Heath claimed her lips once more, whispering between kisses, "We'd better make our engagement very short."

"I agree." Reese laughed and leaned back to examine her ring. She gasped. "It's so beautiful. And it matches my pendant."

Her brows knit together. "Wait a minute... Did you buy this—?"

"A month ago. The same time I bought your birthday gift. I've just been waiting for the right moment."

"And if that moment had never come?"

Heath kissed her then softly said, "I was willing to take the chance that we would get here."

Reese clamped her bottom lip between her teeth as had become her habit when she had something to say but first needed to find the courage. She drew in a long, deep breath. "So, do you have a date in mind?"

"Sometime toward the end of summer? I'd like Hunter to be here, and I'm praying we'll hear any day now about that parole of his." Heath smoothed his hands down her back.

Reese's breath hitched as tingles raced through her body. If that parole didn't come soon, Hunter would have to just miss the wedding.

"Toward the end of summer sounds perfect. But will you be able to wait another three months?" It felt good to be the one teasing for a change.

Heath twined his fingers between hers. "I have waited a lifetime for you. What's another three months or so?"

Reese threw her head back, her laughter filling the sky. "At least ninety days too long. But I'll wait. This time I'll wait."

THE END

GLOSSARY

Bismarck : a fried cruller

Bliant : In the Arthurian legend, Bliant was Selivant's brother who fought Lancelot, but was ultimately defeated. The name Bliant means 'healer'.

Bluff : Direct in speech or behavior but in a good-natured way

BVM : Bag valve mask

Pavé : A setting of stones placed close together so as to show no metal between them [French]

SCRIPTURE REFERENCES

Chapter 2:

Now the serpent was more crafty than any of the wild animals the Lord God had made. He said to the woman, "Did God really say, 'You must not eat from any tree in the garden'?"

The woman said to the serpent, "We may eat fruit from the trees in the garden, but God did say, 'You must not eat fruit from the tree that is in the middle of the garden, and you must not touch it, or you will die.'"

"You will not certainly die," the serpent said to the woman. "For God knows that when you eat from it your eyes will be opened, and you will be like God, knowing good and evil."

When the woman saw that the fruit of the tree was good for food and pleasing to the eye, and also desirable for gaining

wisdom, she took some and ate it. She also gave some to her husband, who was with her, and he ate it. Then the eyes of both of them were opened, and they realized they were naked; so they sewed fig leaves together and made coverings for themselves.
~ Genesis 3 v 1-7

The Parable of the Sower
That same day Jesus went out of the house and sat by the lake. Such large crowds gathered around him that he got into a boat and sat in it, while all the people stood on the shore. Then he told them many things in parables, saying:

"A farmer went out to sow his seed. As he was scattering the seed, some fell along the path, and the birds came and ate it up. Some fell on rocky places, where it did not have much soil. It sprang up quickly, because the soil was shallow. But when the sun came up, the plants were scorched, and they withered because they had no root. Other seed fell among thorns, which grew up and choked the plants. Still other seed fell on good soil, where it produced a crop—a hundred, sixty or thirty times what was sown. Whoever has ears, let them hear."
~ Matthew 13 v 1-9

Chapter 4:

"You have heard that it was said, 'You shall not commit adultery.' But I tell you that anyone who looks at a woman lustfully has already committed adultery with her in his heart."
~ Matthew 5 v 27-28

Chapter 8:

He is the Maker of heaven and earth, the sea, and everything in

them—he remains faithful forever.
~ Psalm 146 v 6

You have searched me, Lord, and you know me. You know when I sit and when I rise; you perceive my thoughts from afar. You discern my going out and my lying down; you are familiar with all my ways. Before a word is on my tongue you, Lord, know it completely. You hem me in behind and before, and you lay your hand upon me. Such knowledge is too wonderful for me, too lofty for me to attain.
~ Psalm 139 v 1-6

Chapter 11:

Love must be sincere. Hate what is evil; cling to what is good. Be devoted to one another in love. Honor one another above yourselves.
~ Romans 12 v 9-10

Do not repay anyone evil for evil. Be careful to do what is right in the eyes of everyone. If it is possible, as far as it depends on you, live at peace with everyone. Do not take revenge, my dear friends, but leave room for God's wrath, for it is written: "It is mine to avenge; I will repay," says the Lord.

On the contrary: "If your enemy is hungry, feed him; if he is thirsty, give him something to drink. In doing this, you will heap burning coals on his head."

Do not be overcome by evil, but overcome evil with good.
~ Romans 12 v 17-21

"You are worthy, our Lord and God, to receive glory and honor and power, for you created all things, and by your will they were

created and have their being."
~ Revelation 4 v 11

Even to your old age and gray hairs I am he, I am he who will sustain you. I have made you and I will carry you; I will sustain you and I will rescue you.
~ Isaiah 46 v 4

Chapter 12:

I have loved you with an everlasting love.
~ Jeremiah 31 v 3

The Lord himself goes before you and will be with you; he will never leave you nor forsake you. Do not be afraid; do not be discouraged. ~ Deuteronomy 31 v 8

Do not be afraid; do not be discouraged.
~ Deuteronomy 1 v 21
~ Deuteronomy 31 v 8
~ Joshua 1 v 9
~ Joshua 8 v 1
~ Joshua 10 v 25
~ 1 Chronicles 22 v 13
~ 1 Chronicles 28 v 20
~ 2 Chronicles 20 v 15, 17
~ 2 Chronicles 32 v 7

…and provide for those who grieve in Zion—to bestow on them a crown of beauty instead of ashes, the oil of joy instead of mourning, and a garment of praise instead of a spirit of despair.
~ Isaiah 61 v 3

For six years you are to sow your fields and harvest the crops, but during the seventh year let the land lie unplowed and unused. Then the poor among your people may get food from it, and the wild animals may eat what is left. Do the same with your vineyard and your olive grove.

~ Exodus 23 v 10-11

Chapter 13:

The Parable of the Lost Sheep
Now the tax collectors and sinners were all gathering around to hear Jesus. But the Pharisees and the teachers of the law muttered, "This man welcomes sinners and eats with them."

Then Jesus told them this parable: "Suppose one of you has a hundred sheep and loses one of them. Doesn't he leave the ninety-nine in the open country and go after the lost sheep until he finds it? And when he finds it, he joyfully puts it on his shoulders and goes home. Then he calls his friends and neighbors together and says, 'Rejoice with me; I have found my lost sheep.' I tell you that in the same way there will be more rejoicing in heaven over one sinner who repents than over ninety-nine righteous persons who do not need to repent.

~ Luke 15 v 1-7

And lead us not into temptation, but deliver us from the evil one.
~ Matthew 6 v 13

Chapter 14:

Be sure to set aside a tenth of all that your fields produce each year.
~ Deuteronomy 14 v 22

Chapter 15:

Because of the Lord's great love we are not consumed, for his compassions never fail. They are new every morning; great is your faithfulness.

~ Lamentations 3 v 22-23

Now to him who is able to do immeasurably more than all we ask or imagine, according to his power that is at work within us, to him be glory in the church and in Christ Jesus throughout all generations, for ever and ever! Amen.

~ Ephesians 3 v 20-21

I hope you enjoyed reading *Remember Me*. If you did, please consider leaving a short review on Amazon, Goodreads, or Bookbub. Positive reviews and word-of-mouth recommendations count as they honor an author and help other readers to find quality Christian fiction to read.

Thank you so much!

Soon you can read *Love Me* (Book 2) by Alexa Verde and *Cherish Me* (Book 3) by Autumn Macarthur. *Choose Me* (Book 4) will release around mid-June 2019. Make sure you don't miss any new releases by following Chapel Cove Romances on Amazon:
https://www.amazon.com/Chapel-Cove-Romances/e/B07PZKWZMR

If you'd like to receive information on new releases, cover reveals, and writing news, please sign up for my newsletter.

http://www.marionueckermann.net/subscribe/

ABOUT MARION UECKERMANN

A Novel Place to Fall in Love

USA Today bestselling author, MARION UECKERMANN's passion for writing was sparked when she moved to Ireland with her family. Her love of travel has influenced her contemporary inspirational romances set in novel places. Marion and her husband again live in South Africa, but with two gorgeous grandsons hanging their hats at the house next door, their empty nest's no longer so empty.

Please visit Marion's website for more of her books:
www.marionueckermann.net

You can also find Marion on social media:
Facebook : Marion.C.Ueckermann

Twitter : ueckie

Goodreads : 5342167.Marion_Ueckermann

Pinterest : ueckie

Bookbub : authors/marion-ueckermann

Amazon : Marion-Ueckermann/e/B00KBYLU7C

TITLES BY MARION UECKERMANN

CHAPEL COVE ROMANCES
Remember Me *(Book 1)*
Choose Me *(Book 4 – Releasing June 2019)*
Accept Me *(Book 7 – Releasing 2019)*
Trust Me *(Book 10 – Releasing May 2020)*
Other books in this tri-author series are by
Alexa Verde and Autumn Macarthur

THE POTTER'S HOUSE
SHAPED BY LOVE
Restoring Faith *(Book 1)*
Recovering Hope *(Book 2)*
Reclaiming Charity *(Book 3)*

A TUSCAN LEGACY
That's Amore *(Book 1)*
Ti Amo *(Book 4)*
Other books in this multi-author series are by: Elizabeth Maddrey, Alexa Verde, Clare
Revell, Heather Gray, Narelle Atkins, and Autumn Macarthur

UNDER THE SUN
SEASONS OF CHANGE
A Time to Laugh *(Book 1)*
A Time to Love *(Book 2)*
A Time to Push Daisies *(Book 3)*

HEART OF ENGLAND
SEVEN SUITORS FOR SEVEN SISTERS
A Match for Magnolia *(Book 1)*
A Romance for Rose *(Book 2)*
A Hero for Heather *(Book 3)*
A Husband for Holly *(Book 4)*
A Courtship for Clover *(Book 5)*
A Love for Lily *(Book 6 – Releasing 2019)*
A Proposal for Poppy *(Book 7 – Releasing 2020)*

HEART OF AFRICA
Orphaned Hearts
The Other You

HEART OF IRELAND
Spring's Promise

HEART OF AUSTRALIA
Melbourne Memories

HEART OF CHRISTMAS
Poles Apart
Ginger & Brad's House

PASSPORT TO ROMANCE
Helsinki Sunrise
Soloppgang i Helsinki
(Norwegian translation of Helsinki Sunrise)
Oslo Overtures
Glasgow Grace

ACFW WRITERS ON THE STORM
SHORT STORY CONTEST WINNERS ANTHOLOGY
Dancing Up A Storm ~ *Dancing In The Rain*

NON-FICTION
Bush Tails
(Humorous & True Short Story Trophies of my Bushveld Escapades
as told by Percival Robert Morrison)

POETRY

GLIMPSES THROUGH POETRY
My Father's Hand
My Savior's Touch
My Colorful Life

WORDS RIPE FOR THE PICKING
Fruit of the Rhyme

When love grows cold and vows forgotten, can faith be restored?

Charles and Faith Young are numbers people. While Charles spends his days in a fancy Fort Collins office number crunching, Faith teaches math to the students of Colorado High. Married for sixteen years, Charles and Faith both know unequivocally that one plus one should never equal three.

When blame becomes the order of the day in the Young household for their failing marriage—blaming each other, blaming themselves—Charles and Faith each search for answers why the flame of love no longer burns brightly. In their efforts, one takes comfort from another a step too far. One chooses not to get mad, but to get even.

Dying love is a slow burn. Is it too late for Charles and Faith to fan the embers and make love rise once again from the ashes of their broken marriage? Can they find their first love again—for each other, and for God?

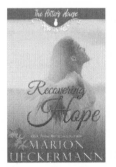

In a single moment, a dream dies, and hope is lost.

Lovers of the ocean, Hope and Tyler Peterson long for the day they can dip their little one's feet into its clear blue waters and pass on their passion for the sea.

Despite dedicating her life to the rescue and rehabilitation of God's sea creatures, when their dream dies, Hope can't muster the strength to do the same for herself. Give her a dark hole to hide away from the world and she'd be happy…if happiness were ever again within her reach.

While Tyler is able to design technology that probes the mysteries of the deep, he's at a loss to find a way to help Hope surface from the darkness that has dragged her into its abyss. He struggles to plan for their future when his wife can barely cope with the here and now.

If they can't recover hope, their marriage won't survive.

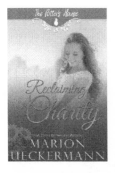

Some artworks appear chaotic, but it all depends on the eye of the beholder.

Brody and Madison Peterson have the picture-perfect marriage. Or so it seems. But their teenage daughter Charity knows only too well that that's not the case. Frequent emotive arguments—the bane of artistic temperaments—have Charity pouring out her heartache and fears in her prayer journal.

When Madison makes a career choice that doesn't fit in with her husband's plans for their lives or their art gallery, disaster looms. The end of their marriage and a bitter battle over Charity threatens.

What will it take for the Master Artist to heal old wounds and transform their broken marriage into a magnificent masterpiece? Could Charity's journal be enough to make Brody and Madison realize their folly and reclaim their love?

For thirty years, Brian and Elizabeth Dunham have served on the mission field. Unable to have children of their own, they've been a father and mother to countless orphans in six African countries. When an unexpected beach-house inheritance and a lung disease diagnosis coincide, they realize that perhaps God is telling them it's time to retire.

At sixty, Elizabeth is past child-bearing age. She'd long ago given up wondering whether this would be the month she would conceive. But when her best friend and neighbor jokes that Elizabeth's sudden fatigue and nausea are symptoms of pregnancy, Elizabeth finds herself walking that familiar and unwanted road again, wondering if God is pulling an Abraham and Sarah on her and Brian.

The mere notion has questions flooding Elizabeth's mind. If she were miraculously pregnant, would they have the stamina to raise a child in their golden years? Especially with Brian's health issues. And the child? Would it be healthy, or would it go through life struggling with some kind of disability? What of her own health? Could she survive giving birth?

Will what Brian and Elizabeth have dreamed of their entire married life be an old-age blessing or a curse?

Everyday life for Dr. Melanie Kerr had consisted of happy deliveries and bundles of joy…until her worst nightmare became reality. The first deaths in her OR during an emergency C-section. Both mother and child, one month before Christmas. About to perform her first Caesarean since the tragedy, Melanie loses her nerve and flees the OR. She packs her bags and catches a flight to Budapest. Perhaps time spent in the city her lost patient hailed from, can help her find the healing and peace she desperately needs to be a good doctor again.

Since the filming of Jordan's Journeys' hit TV serial "Life Begins at Sixty" ended earlier in the year, journalist and TV host Jordan Stanson has gone from one assignment to the next. But before he can take a break, he has a final episode to film—"Zac's First Christmas". Not only is he looking forward to relaxing at his parents' seaside home, he can't wait to see his godchild, Zac, the baby born to the aging Dunhams. His boss, however, has squeezed in another documentary for him to complete before Christmas—uncovering the tragedy surrounding the doctor the country came to love on his show, the beautiful Dr. Kerr.

In order to chronicle her journey through grief and failure, Jordan has no choice but to get close to this woman. Something he has both tried and failed at in the past. He hopes through this assignment, he'll be able to help her realize the tragedy wasn't her fault. But even in a city so far away from home, work once again becomes the major catalyst to hinder romance between Jordan and Melanie.

That, and a thing called honesty.

Not every woman is fortunate enough to find her soulmate. Fewer find him twice.

JoAnn Stanson has loved and lost. Widowed a mere eighteen months ago, JoAnn is less than thrilled when her son arranges a luxury cruise around the British Isles as an early birthday gift. She's not ready to move on and "meet new people".

Caleb Blume has faced death and won. Had it not been for an unexpected Christmas present, he would surely have been pushing up daisies. Not that the silver-haired landscape architect was averse to those little flowers—he just wasn't ready to become fertilizer himself.

To celebrate his sixty-fourth birthday and the nearing two-year anniversary since he'd cheated death, Caleb books a cruise and flies to London. He is instantly drawn in a way that's never happened before to a woman he sees boarding the ship. But this woman who steals Caleb's heart is far more guarded with her own.

For JoAnn, so many little things about Caleb remind her of her late husband. It's like loving the same man twice. Yet different.

When Rafaele and Jayne meet again two years after dancing the night away together in Tuscany, is it a matter of fate or of faith?

After deciding to take a six-month sabbatical, Italian lawyer Rafaele Rossi moves from Florence back to Villa Rossi in the middle of Tuscany, resigned to managing the family farm for his aging nonna after his father's passing. Convinced a family get-together is what Nonna needs to lift her spirits, he plans an eightieth birthday party for her, making sure his siblings and cousins attend.

The Keswick jewelry store where Jayne Austin has worked for seven years closes its doors. Jayne takes her generous severance pay and heads off to Italy—Tuscany to be precise. Choosing to leave her fate in God's hands, she prays she'll miraculously bump into the handsome best man she'd danced the night away with at a friend's Tuscan wedding two years ago. She hasn't been able to forget those smoldering brown eyes and that rich Italian accent.

Jayne's prayers are answered swiftly and in the most unexpected way. Before she knows what's happening, she's a guest not only at Isabella Rossi's birthday party, but at Villa Rossi too.

When Rafaele receives what appears to be a valuable painting from an unknown benefactor, he's reminded that he doesn't want to lose Jayne again. After what he's done to drive her from the villa, though, what kind of a commitment will it take for her to stay?

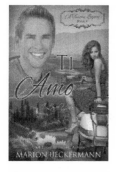

She never wants to get married. He does. To her.

The day Alessandra Rossi was born, her mammà died, and a loveless life with the father who blamed the newborn for her mother's death followed. With the help of her oldest brother, Rafaele, Alessa moved away from home the moment she finished school— just like her other siblings had. Now sporting a degree in architectural history and archaeology, Alessa loves her job as a tour guide in the city of Rome—a place where she never fails to draw the attention of men. Not that Alessa cares. Fearing that the man she weds would be anything like her recently deceased father has Alessa vowing to remain single.

American missionary Michael Young has moved to Rome on a two-year mission trip. His temporary future in the country doesn't stop him from spontaneously joining Alessa's tour after spotting her outside the Colosseum. *And* being bold enough to tell her afterward that one day she'd be his wife. God had told him. And he believed Him. But Alessa shows no sign of interest in Michael.

Can anything sway the beautiful and headstrong Italian to fall in love? Can anyone convince her to put her faith and hope in the Heavenly Father, despite being raised by an earthly one who never loved her? Will her sister's prompting, or a mysterious painting, or Michael himself change Alessa's mind? About love. And about God.

Womanizer. Adulterer. Divorced. That is Lord Davis Rathbone's history. His future? He vows to never marry or fall in love again—repeating his past mistakes, not worth the risk. Then he meets Magnolia Blume, and filling his days penning poetry no longer seems an alternative to channel his pent-up feelings. With God's help, surely he can keep this rare treasure and make it work this time?

Magnolia Blume's life is perfect, except for one thing—Davis Rathbone is everything she's not looking for in a man. He doesn't strike her as one prone to the sentiments of family, or religion, but her judgments could be premature.

Magnolia must look beyond the gossip, Davis's past, and their differences to find her perfect match, because, although flawed, Davis has one redeeming quality—he is a man after God's own heart.

Rose Blume has a secret, and she's kept it for six long years. It's the reason she's convinced herself she'll have to find her joy making wedding dresses, and not wearing one.

Fashion design icon Joseph Digiavoni crosses paths with Rose for the first time since their summer romance in Florence years before, and all the old feelings for her come rushing back. Not that they ever really left. He's lived with her image since she returned to England.

Joseph and Rose are plunged into working together on the wedding outfits for the upcoming Rathbone / Blume wedding. His top client is marrying Rose's sister. But will this task prove too difficult, especially when Joseph is anxious for Rose to admit why she broke up with him in Italy and what she'd done in the months that followed?

One person holds the key to happiness for them all, if only Rose and Joseph trusted that the truth would set them free. When they finally do bare their secrets, who has the most to forgive?

Paxton Rathbone is desperate to make his way home. His inheritance long spent, he stows away on a fishing trawler bound from Norway to England only to be discovered, beaten and discarded at Scarborough's port. On home soil at last, all it would take is one phone call. But even if his mother and father are forgiving, he doubts his older brother will be.

Needing a respite from child welfare social work, Heather Blume is excited about a short-term opportunity to work at a busy North Yorkshire day center for the homeless. When one of the men she's been helping saves her from a vicious attack, she's so grateful she violates one of the most important rules in her profession—she takes him home to tend his wounds. But there's more to her actions than merely being the Good Samaritan. The man's upper-crust speech has Heather intrigued. She has no doubt he's a gentleman fallen far from grace and is determined to reunite the enigmatic young man with his family, if only he would open up about his life.

Paxton has grown too accustomed to the disdain of mankind, which perhaps is why Heather's kindness penetrates his reserves and gives him reason to hope. Reason to love? Perhaps reason to stay. But there's a fine line between love and gratitude, for both Paxton and Heather.

Holly Blume loves decorating people's homes, but that doesn't mean she's ready to play house.

Believing a house is not a home without a woman's touch, there's nothing more Reverend Christopher Stewart would like than to find a wife. What woman would consider him marriage material, though, with an aging widowed father to look after, especially one who suffers from Alzheimer's?

When Christopher arrives at his new parish, he discovers the church ladies have arranged a welcome surprise—an office makeover by congregant and interior designer Holly Blume. Impressed with Miss Blume's work, Christopher decides to contract the talented lady to turn the rectory into a home. When they begin to clash more than their taste in color, will the revamp come to the same abrupt end as his only romantic relationship?

Despite their differences, Holly resolves to finish the job of redesigning the Stewart home, while Christopher determines to re-form Holly's heart.

Top London chef Clover Blume has one chance to become better acquainted with Jonathan Spalding away from the mayhem of her busy restaurant where he frequently dines—usually with a gorgeous woman at his side. When the groomsman who is supposed to escort her at her sister's New Year's Eve wedding is delayed because of business, Clover begins to wonder whether she really wants to waste time with a player whose main focus in life is making money rather than keeping promises.

Jonathan lives the good life. There's one thing, however, the London Investment Banker's money hasn't managed to buy: a woman to love—one worthy of his mother's approval. Is it possible though, that the auburn-haired beauty who is to partner with him at his best friend's wedding—a wedding he stands to miss thanks to a glitch in a deal worth millions—is finding a way into his heart?

But what will it cost Jonathan to realize it profits him nothing to gain the world, yet lose his soul?

And the girl.

 Who am I? The question has Taylor Cassidy journeying from one side of America to the other seeking an answer. Almost five years brings her no closer to the truth. Now an award-winning photojournalist for Wines & Vines, Taylor is sent on assignment to South Africa to discover the inspiration behind Aimee Amour, the DeBois estate's flagship wine. Mystery has enshrouded the story of the woman for whom the wine is named.

South African winegrower Armand DeBois's world is shattered when a car accident leaves him in a coma for three weeks, and his young wife dead. The road of recovery and mourning is dark, and Armand teeters between falling away from God and falling into His comforting arms.

When Armand and Taylor meet, questions arise for them both. While the country and the winegrower hold a strange attraction for Taylor, Armand struggles with the uncertainty of whether he's falling in love with his past or his future.

 When his wife dies in childbirth, conservationist Simon Hartley pours his life into raising his daughter and his orphan elephants. He has no time, or desire, to fall in love again. Or so he thinks.

Wanting to escape English society and postpone an arranged marriage, Lady Abigail Chadwick heads to Africa for a year to teach the children of the Good Shepherd Orphanage. Upon her arrival she is left stranded at Livingstone airport…until a reluctant Simon comes to her rescue.

Now only fears born of his loss, and secrets of the life she's tried to leave behind, can stonewall their romance, budding in the heart of Africa.

Escaping his dangerous past, former British rock star Justin "The Phoenix" Taylor flees as far away from home as possible to Australia. A marked man with nothing left but his guitar and his talent, Justin is desperate to start over yet still live off the grid. Loneliness and the need to feel a connection to the London pastor who'd saved his life draw Justin to Ella's Barista Art Coffee Shop—the famous and trendy Melbourne establishment belonging to Pastor Jim Anderson's niece.

Intrigued by the bearded stranger who looks vaguely familiar, Ella Anderson wearies of serving him his regular flat white espresso every morning with no more than a greeting for conversation. Ella decides to discover his secrets, even if it requires coaxing him with her elaborate latte art creations. And muffins.

Justin gradually begins to open up to Ella but fears his past will collide with their future. When it does, Ella must decide whether they have a future at all.

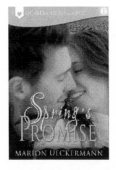

1972. Every day in Belfast, Northern Ireland, holds risk, especially for the mayor's daughter. But Dr. Olivia O'Hare has a heart for people and chooses to work on the wrong side of a city where colors constantly clash. The orange and green of the Republicans pitted against the red and blue of those loyal to Britain. While they might share the common hue of white, it brings no peace.

Caught between the Republicans and Loyalists' conflict, blue-collar worker Ryann Doyle has to wonder if there's life before death. The answer seems to be a resounding, 'No'. His mother is dead, his father's a drunk, and his younger brother, Declan, is steeped in the Provisional IRA. Then he crosses paths with Olivia O'Hare.

After working four days straight, mopping up PIRA's latest act of terror, Olivia is exhausted. All she wants is to go home and rest. But when she drives away from Royal Victoria Hospital, rest is the last thing Olivia gets.

When Declan kidnaps the Lord Mayor of Belfast's daughter, Ryann has to find a way to rescue the dark-haired beauty, though it means he must turn his back on his own flesh and blood for someone he just met.

 While Ginger Murphy completes her music studies, childhood sweetheart and neighbor, Brad O'Sullivan betrays her with the new girl next door. Heartbroken, Ginger escapes as far away as she can go—to Australia—for five long years. During this time, Brad's shotgun marriage fails. Besides his little boy, Jamie, one other thing in his life has turned out sweet and successful—his pastry business.

When her mother's diagnosed with heart failure, Ginger has no choice but to return to the green grass of Ireland. As a sought-after wedding flautist, she quickly establishes herself on home soil. Although she loves her profession, she fears she'll never be more than the entertainment at these joyous occasions. And that she's doomed to bump into the wedding cake chef she tries to avoid. Brad broke her heart once. She won't give him a chance to do it again.

A gingerbread house contest at church to raise funds for the homeless has Ginger competing with Brad. Both are determined to win—Ginger the contest, Brad her heart. But when a dear old saint challenges that the Good Book says the first shall be last, and the last first, Ginger has to decide whether to back down from contending with Brad and embrace the true meaning of Christmas—peace on earth, good will to all men. Even the Irishman she'd love to hate.

Writer's block and a looming Christmas novel deadline have romance novelist, Sarah Jones, heading for the other side of the world on a whim.

Niklas Toivonen offers cozy Lapland accommodation, but when his aging father falls ill, Niklas is called upon to step into his father's work clothes to make children happy. Red is quite his color.

Fresh off the airplane, a visit to Santa sets Sarah's muse into overdrive. The man in red is not only entertaining, he's young—with gorgeous blue eyes. Much like her new landlord's, she discovers. Santa and Niklas quickly become objects of research—for her novel, and her curiosity.

Though she's written countless happily-ever-afters, Sarah doubts she'll ever enjoy her own. Niklas must find a way to show her how to leave the pain of her past behind, so she can find love and faith once more.

Opera singer, Skye Hunter, returns to the land of her birth as leading lady in Phantom of the Opera. This is her first trip back to bonnie Scotland since her mother whisked her away to Australia after Skye's father died sixteen years ago.

When Skye decides to have dinner at McGuire's, she's not going there only for Mary McGuire's shepherd's pie. Her first and only love, Callum McGuire, still plays his guitar and sings at the family-owned tavern.

Callum has never stopped loving Skye. Desperate to know if she's changed under her mother's influence, he keeps his real profession hidden. Would she want him if he was still a singer in a pub? But when Skye's worst nightmare comes true, Callum reveals his secret to save the woman he loves.

Can Skye and Callum rekindle what they lost, or will her mother threaten their future together once again?

"If women were meant to fly, the skies would be pink."

Those were the first words Anjelica Joergensen heard from renowned wingsuiter, Kyle Sheppard, when they joined an international team in Oslo to break the formation flying Guinness World Record. This wouldn't be the last blunder Kyle would make around the beautiful Norwegian.

The more Anjelica tries to avoid Kyle, the more the universe pushes them together. Despite their awkward start, she finds herself reluctantly attracted to the handsome New Zealander. But beneath his saintly exterior, is Kyle just another daredevil looking for the next big thrill?

Falling for another wingsuiter would only be another love doomed.

When a childhood sweetheart comes between them, Kyle makes a foolish agreement which jeopardizes the event and endangers his life, forcing Anjelica to make a hard choice.

Is she the one who'll clip his wings?

Can he be the wind beneath hers?

Three weeks alone at a friend's summer cottage on a Finnish lake to fast and pray. That was Adam Carter's plan. But sometimes plans go awry.

On an impromptu trip to her family's secluded summer cottage, the last thing Eveliina Mikkola expected to find was a missionary from the other side of the world—in her sauna.

Determined to stay, Eveliina will do whatever it takes—from shortcrust pastry to shorts—to send the man of God packing. This island's too small for them both.

Adam Carter, however, is not about to leave.

Will he be able to resist her temptations?

Can she withstand his prayers?

 Their outdoor wedding planned for the middle of Africa's rainy summer, chances are it'll pour on Mirabelle Kelly's bridal parade—after all, she is marrying Noah Raines.

To make matters worse, the African Rain Queen, Modjadji, is invited to the wedding.

Mirabelle must shun her superstitions and place her faith in the One who really controls the weather.

Made in the USA
Columbia, SC
14 September 2019